The Summer Invitation

The Summer Invitation

Charlotte Silver

Roaring Brook Press
New York

Acknowledgments

Much gratitude goes to my agent, Emily Forland, and to my editor, Nancy Mercado, as well as to Angie Chen and the wonderful team at Roaring Brook. And special thanks to the late, great Lindy Hess, who first suggested that I write a young adult book, and to Jane O'Reilly, who made my summer chaperoning gig happen.

Text copyright © 2014 by Charlotte Silver
Map and ornament art copyright © 2014 by Sarah Watts
Published by Roaring Brook Press
Roaring Brook Press is a division of Holtzbrinck Publishing Holdings Limited Partnership
175 Fifth Avenue, New York, New York 10010
macteenbooks.com

Library of Congress Cataloging-in-Publication Data
Silver, Charlotte.
    The summer invitation / Charlotte Silver. — First edition.
      pages cm
    Summary: When Franny and her older sister Valentine are summoned by their aunt Theodora from foggy San Francisco to sunny New York City for one summer, they unearth secrets about Aunt Theo's romantic past and even have a few romantic adventures of their own.
    ISBN 978-1-59643-829-3 (hardcover)
    ISBN 978-1-59643-830-9 (e-book)
    [1. Coming of age—Fiction.   2. Sisters—Fiction.   3. Love—Fiction.   4. Summer—Fiction.   5. New York (N.Y.)—Fiction.]   I. Title.

PZ7.S585654Su 2014
[Fic]—dc23
                                        2013044976

Roaring Brook Press books may be purchased for business or promotional use. For information on bulk purchases please contact Macmillan Corporate and Premium Sales Department at (800) 221-7945 x5442 or by email at specialmarkets@macmillan.com.

First edition, 2014
Book design by Roberta Pressel
Printed in the United States of America

10 9 8 7 6 5 4 3 2 1

To E & R

Our Man...

♡ BARGEMUSIC ♡

Caffe Reggio

WASHINGTON SQUARE PARK

GRA
TR
Oy.

Brooklyn

Table of Contents

The Summer Invitation

Prologue

Aunt Theodora Invites Us

Aunt Theodora's invitation arrived all the way from Paris on a piece of French stationery. The edges were scalloped and her handwriting on the lavender-colored paper was black and slashing, like a sword. It read:

Dear Frances and Valentine,

Has your mother ever told you that once upon a time I warned her in no uncertain terms against moving to San Francisco? I visited the place just once in my life and I was so bored I could weep! An old admirer of mine thought he would woo me by taking me on a tour of wine country. The fool. Had he been paying attention, he might have known I only ever drink Italian reds or French champagnes.

The entire state of California is for people who talk too slow. And if one is craving sunshine, which I admit one sometimes does, one goes abroad for that. Italy is just the ticket. Failing that, Greece.

You are young ladies now and I don't like to think of you just chilling, as they say, in San Francisco.

So, I am commanding your mother to let you come to New York this summer and stay in my apartment in Greenwich Village. Not Italy, but almost. This offer will not be repeated.

I know that your parents wouldn't be keen on letting you stay in the apartment alone, so my friend Clover Leslie has agreed to act as your chaperone for the first month while I'm away and I shall join you after that. Don't worry, Clover is not an old lady, and do not fear that you will have to address her as "Miss Leslie." She is twenty-eight and can teach you some things because she learned everything she knows from me.

So it's arranged???

Life unfolds.

XXX
Theo

1

The Umbrellas of San Francisco

Aunt Theodora isn't our *real* aunt, though. She's just this older woman who Mom got to know in Paris and has been friends with ever since. Aunt Theodora has lived the whole world over—we get postcards and letters postmarked from New York or Paris or Budapest or Rome—but she was born in Boston to one of those old families that had something to do with founding the country way back. Her full name is Theodora Wentworth Whitin Bell, and I guess in Boston all those names are supposed to be a big deal. I don't know about that; I just know I like the sounds of them. *Theodora. Wentworth. Whitin. Bell.*

Aunt Theo is old-fashioned, and proud of it. She doesn't *do* e-mail. She rarely *does* the phone. She doesn't *do* a lot of things, but she does do letters. Not predictable birthday and Christmas cards with tidy little checks like what other older relatives send you. And never cards from the drugstore with a vase of flowers on the front and cute sayings inside. No, just letters, arriving out of the blue on a random crummy day and giving you a little lift. I always look forward to them. Val says: "Didn't Aunt Theodora get the memo that *nobody* sends letters anymore?"

The only time Val and I ever send letters is when Mom makes us write thank-you notes after we get presents on Christmas and our birthdays. But still, I like getting letters even though I don't send them that often. Letters are special, and especially Aunt Theo's.

Valentine was born in Paris and nobody knows who her father is. She has copper curls and violet eyes. Mom says not to call them violet, just dark blue. But that's because Mom has the same eyes and she's too modest to call them violet, which sounds *so dramatic*. Violet is one of my favorite words.

When Mom was a young woman, she moved to Paris after graduate school and worked for some famous Italian architect. His big thing was designing opera houses around the world. Everybody used to say she looked just like Elizabeth Taylor, that old actress with the violet eyes and all the ex-husbands.

It's so unfair. Valentine's name is French, and mine is only English. Mom likes for people to pronounce Valentine in the French fashion, so the last syllable rhymes with *lean* rather than *line*. Say it to yourself: *Valentine*. Oh, it's another lovely sounding word. I should tell you right away though that Mom isn't of French heritage or anything like that, just a Francophile, she says. We go to French school, where pronouncing Valentine's name right is not a problem, and where some of our classmates are named things like Isabelle, Thérèse, and Celeste. But outside of school, people get it wrong, even though Mom has this stern way of saying "And this is my daughter Valen*tine*" with an emphasis on the last syllable. Actually, though, she only started going by Valentine recently. It used to be that everybody but Mom called her Val, which I think still suits her much better, but don't tell her that. Mom always insisted on the full name because that way you can tell it's

French. Her eyes used to just snap whenever a new person addressed Valentine as Val instead.

Mom's eyes can really snap because, just like Elizabeth Taylor, she also has these dramatic, satiny black eyebrows. I wish I had them too, but so far, there is nothing too dramatic to report about *me*. Mom always says I have chestnut hair but I know I don't. I know it's just plain mousy. And it's *straight*. I know some girls like straight hair these days, but I think curly is much prettier. Val can put her hair up in this big twist with the curls slipping out up front, and it's so pretty. She knows it too! She'll practice sweeping up her hair in front of the mirror when she thinks I'm not looking.

I was born three years after Val in San Francisco, and my father is Val's stepfather; he adopted her so now we all have the same last name. Well anyway, Mom and Dad got married when Val was so young, he might just as well be her real father. Dad works in real estate and is big on the opera. He's the type of father who's always trying to educate you at the dinner table. Sometimes I get the feeling Mom is kind of bored with him, but maybe that's just what marriage is like. But he's very nice to us and pays for the fancy school we go to. Mom is an architect who designs wineries in Napa Valley. We live in one of those Victorian houses with all the crazy colors in Pacific Heights. Peacock-blue door, rose trim on the windows. That's where I was born. A home birth, Mom always says, like it was this really great thing.

Valentine was born in a hospital somewhere in Paris and Mom was all alone. But that's another story.

When we were little, Mom used to tell us stories of her life in Paris as a young woman, and then she would break off in the middle and sigh.

The mystery of who Val's father might have been was the only thing in our lives that was the least bit romantic. When Mom and Dad weren't there, we talked about him all the time. The story of the circumstances surrounding Valentine's birth was like a favorite story we'd listen to again and again at bedtime, changing certain details to suit our mood. Sometimes her father was a penniless artist in a garret. Other times we wanted him to be wildly rich and own a chateau stocked with the most fabulous wine cellar. Not that we drink wine—*yet*.

Oh, I forgot to mention that Valentine and I are both really into singing. Mom and Dad saw to it that we took lessons, though we like to sing just about anything really, silly songs and new songs too. We sing in the San Francisco Girls Chorus. On rainy days when we were little Mom would always play an old record of the sound track to *The Umbrellas of Cherbourg—Les Parapluies de Cherbourg*—and make us sing along. That's our favorite movie because the songs are in French and it has all of these crazy bright colors; you could just eat it up, that movie's so yummy-looking. One day Valentine stopped singing and asked:

"Is that what it's like?"

"What?" said Mom.

"Being in love."

And Mom sighed and said, "No, not really."

The day Aunt Theo's invitation arrived it was a Saturday morning and we were eating breakfast. During the week, we always eat breakfast in the kitchen, and Dad's so busy that by the time Val and I get up he's already at work. But on Saturdays and Sundays we all sit at the dining room table with the French paperweights on it. Dad makes our favorite breakfast, which is Nutella crepes and fresh-squeezed tangerine juice. Mom and Dad drink coffee, of course, which I would love to drink too (with plenty of sugar!), but we're only ever allowed to drink it when we're in Europe. Because I guess in Europe anything can happen.

Mom held up the mystery letter and said, "Girls, who do you think this is from?"

"Who?" I asked, looking at the letter. Val wasn't paying the least bit attention. She was too busy spreading her crepe with *gobs and gobs* of Nutella. I put just a neat layer of Nutella and fold the crepe and sprinkle it with powdered sugar. Val puts powdered sugar, plus she squeezes a tangerine over it so the juices are all running.

But as soon as I glanced at the envelope, I guessed who it was from. Aunt Theo's handwriting is inky and dramatic, like Mom's eyebrows. She always has the most gorgeous stationery, heavy, with hand-cut scalloped edges. I think it's always the same brand of stationery, French stationery, but she uses different colors. It's never girly or happy colors with Aunt Theo, never those wonderful candy-box colors like they have in *The Umbrellas of Cherbourg*. It's always rich, sorrowful colors, deep purples, coffee browns, dusty reds. They're a woman's colors.

"I have a question," I said. "Why, if Aunt Theo's such a big traveler, doesn't she ever come and visit us?"

"Oh, but she hates Northern California," said Mom, laughing. "It's one of her positions in life. Hating Northern California."

"But *we're* here," I protested.

"Theodora Bell is a woman of inflexible principles, Franny," Dad said.

Then Val made a good point: "But that doesn't make any sense. I thought most East Coast people even if they disliked California still liked *Northern* California. I mean, everybody loves San Francisco."

"Valentine! Theodora Bell is not everybody."

"Oh, please," said Val, with a roll of violet eyes. And she went back to eating her crepe. Which meant that I got to read the letter first.

"Oh my God, this is so exciting!" I announced.

"What is?" said Val, finally paying attention. And when she got to the end of the letter, she too said right away: "Oh my God, Franny's right. This is so exciting!"

"What is?" Mom wanted to know.

"New York City!" Val burst out.

"New York City?" said Mom.

"New York City?" said Dad.

So then he took the letter from Val, and Mom read it over his shoulder, like couples do.

"Well," she said afterward, "that's Theo all over. I suppose you're dying to go?"

"Now, now—" Dad began, in the voice that means: *not so fast.*

"Oh, Edward, but Theo's arranged it so perfectly," said Mom. "They're going to have a *chaperone.* And we've met Clover before. In Paris once, don't you remember?"

"I remember," said Dad.

"Clover Leslie is a lovely young woman and I'm sure she'll be a most responsible chaperone," said Mom. "I feel all right sending the girls away if they'll be staying with somebody we know. You thought she was lovely, Edward, remember. Remember," she kept on saying, really begging him to let us go.

Meanwhile, Valentine was getting carried away, as if our parents had already said we could go, no questions asked.

"New York City!" exclaimed Valentine. "New York City! An apartment in the Village! Oh, just wait till I tell my friends. They're going to be sooo jealous."

"*Valentine,*" began Mom, to admonish her for being bratty.

But Valentine didn't listen. Instead she leaned over and whispered into my ear, "There will be cute boys there," and I started to feel a little bit left out because I could already imagine a whole summer ahead of us in which she would be more excited about meeting cute boys in New York City than hanging out with me.

"Well, Edward?" said Mom. "What do you think?" It was clear that she already had decided to let us go, but then Mom can be kind of a pushover. Still, I could tell that she really did want us to get to go, because she said: "Remember, Theodora Bell was such a great influence on me when I was a young woman, and I'd love for her to be an influence on the girls' life too. Also"—she reached for the letter across the table and skimmed it again—"it says that she'll be joining Clover in New York the middle of August. So, she'll be there too! The girls will get to meet her."

By the end of breakfast, we'd all convinced Dad to say yes. I think it was the idea of us having a chaperone for part of the time that sold him. He remarked that Aunt Theo's unusual proposal sounded like a very "educational" experiment. And Mom said: "Girls, it will be a summer to remember all your life."

2

The Bluebird of Greenwich Village

*T*he previous three summers, Val and I had gone to a music camp. We were sorry to miss it because we liked all the friends we'd made there, but no way would we give up the opportunity to go to New York.

"A program," exclaimed Val. "A program! Who wants that? That's like being *in school*. We're going to have adventures. In *New York City*. We're going to Live!"

I hoped so. Oh, how I hoped so! When you're fourteen or even seventeen, it seems like you're just waiting for Life with a Capital L to happen.

Meanwhile, every night at dinner, Mom and Dad drank wine and discussed Aunt Theo. She was our main subject of conversation in the days leading up to our trip.

Dad told us: "She used to be one of the great beauties of the age."

"From a long line of beauties," said Mom, and reminded us that Theo's ancestors had been painted by John Singer Sargent, whose painting *Portrait of Madame X* of a redhead in a black velvet gown we once studied at school.

"And when she was at Radcliffe," Dad chimed in, "she was on the cover of *Mademoiselle*. The college girl issue. Do they still do that issue anymore?"

"Edward!" exclaimed Mom, giggling. "I don't even think that *Mademoiselle* exists anymore, does it? Let alone the college girl issue. Oh dear! We must be getting old."

Now they both laughed, which is something I've noticed that grownups do when speaking of getting old, as if it were funny. But is it?

"And then after Radcliffe, of course, she was an Avedon model," said Dad, trying to draw Val and me back into the grownup conversation.

"A *what* model?" asked Val.

"Avedon. Richard Avedon. He was *the* fashion photographer of the age."

"Very chic," said Mom. "Why—girls! Remember that movie *Funny Face*?" We both love Audrey Hepburn, so of course we did. That's the one where she's a bookstore clerk in Greenwich Village who gets discovered to be a model and goes to Paris. "Well. The Fred Astaire character was based on him."

"Oh," we said, swooning. We just loved musicals.

"Aunt Theo used to have a lot of boyfriends, right?" said Val. Being seventeen, this was her idea of the most important thing.

Mom paused and said thoughtfully: "Yes, though she wouldn't have called them boyfriends, which, come to think of it, is not a very attractive or romantic word. She would have called them lovers."

Lovers: I said the word to myself, just in my head. I would have been embarrassed to say it out loud. *Lovers*. Lovers plural! Just imagine it! I was at the age where a lot of my friends had had their first kisses, and some of them were even starting to have boyfriends, but I have to confess: I'd never even been kissed. Maybe this summer, I thought. Maybe in New York . . .

"The worst kind of heartbreaker," said Dad. "Remember that story about what happened to that one boyfriend, Red Lyman, the Harvard quarterback who attempted suicide . . ."

"*Edward*," said Mom, in the voice that meant: *not in front of the girls.*

The night before we left for New York, our last night at home with Mom and Dad for a long time, we all watched this movie that Aunt Theo was in when she was young and living in Hollywood for a time. The movie was from the late 1960s, Dad said. Aunt Theo played a sexy co-ed wearing a long black graduation gown and got to kiss a very famous movie star. It's true that she was as beautiful as everybody said. Not pretty—beautiful. But to me, you know what Aunt Theo looked like? *Like a cross between an angel and a witch.*

~ ◇ ~

Early the next morning, we got to fly to New York by ourselves. It was the first plane flight I'd ever been on without Mom and Dad, and I felt so light and free! Then we took a cab to Aunt Theo's, which felt like a very dashing and independent thing to do. In San Francisco, we hardly ever have any reason to take cabs. But in New York City, they're such a wonderful yellow, just like in the movies, like the yolk of a very rich egg.

Aunt Theo's apartment was on the seventeenth floor of this huge building on what Mom and Dad said was referred to as "Lower Fifth." Dad said, "Leave it to Theodora Bell to have the most exclusive address in New York City," but you wouldn't know this just to look at it because a lot of the buildings we saw were much more la-di-da than Theo's. I mean all the really shiny renovated ones jutting into the sky, where you know they have newly glazed bathtubs and new flat-screen televisions and new everything.

Theo's building wasn't like that. Theo's building was like a big crumbling piece of wedding cake; it was this pale yellow stone, almost the color of butterscotch, and the windows had white molding, which maked me think of frosting. Inside, the floors in the lobby were brown-and-white diamond parquet, and then there was this wallpaper that was thick chocolate-and-navy stripes.

The head doorman was named Oscar, and right away we decided he must be Viennese. He wore bow ties, which are something you never see anyone wear in California. Miss Bell's apartment, he called it, as in "Ah yes, Miss Frances and Miss Valentine! You are the young ladies who will be staying in Miss Bell's apartment."

"Why, after you, Miss Frances," said Valentine as we got in the elevator. I felt at once that she was making fun of me. Evidently Oscar had gotten the memo from Aunt Theo to call me Frances, not Franny.

"After you, Miss Valentine," I said.

"But Miss Valentine sounds *way* cooler than Miss Frances and you know it."

Aunt Theo's apartment was one of those really cool ones where the elevator opens right onto the apartment itself. We'd never seen anything like that before! You don't ever have to see your neighbors in the hallway, just riding in the elevator, I guess.

That was the first surprise. The second one was meeting

Clover Leslie, our chaperone. She was there waiting for us in front of the elevator right away. We hugged her and she hugged us back, as if she had known us forever. She looked at our suitcases and then said, as casually as if the three of us were already friends and happened to be in the middle of some ongoing conversation: "But don't you have any dresses? Trust me, dresses are the way to go in New York in the summer. You're not going to believe how hot it gets here. You're going to *perish* of exhaustion."

Perish. That was the type of word Clover used. I could tell from the way she spoke that she *had* learned a lot from Aunt Theo. In some ways they were really quite different, but they had this striking way of expressing themselves. Even though I'd never met Aunt Theo in person, I could tell exactly how she spoke from the tone of her letters.

"What do you think Clover will be like?" I had asked Valentine, back when we were still in San Francisco.

"I don't know, I'm just glad she's not old."

"Twenty-eight's pretty old."

"Not old *old*, silly."

It was, to me. Old enough that I could not quite imagine being it myself someday. When I thought about it, I only ever got to twenty-one or twenty-two. I could imagine going away to college, but not graduating from college. I couldn't figure out what one would have to look forward to after that.

Back in San Francisco, Dad had made the mistake of asking Aunt Theo if she could send us a picture of Clover. Theo dashed off a brisk little postcard admonishing him:

No pictures. This summer let mystery prevail. Basta!

XXX

Theo

Valentine said, "I hope she's very beautiful."

I was doubtful that there was so much beauty in the world, what with us already knowing Theo the former Avedon model and all.

"Maybe."

"Well, you have to be good-looking to live in New York City. And thin! That too."

Clover, as it turned out when we finally met her, was small. She had the same shape figure Valentine's getting, with the boobs and the tiny waist and all, but she was short: I could tell she'd have to watch it a bit, say if she ate too many pastries. Valentine's five foot nine now and I'm five foot seven, and it's funny because we both towered over her even though she was supposed to be our chaperone. Also, she didn't look anywhere near twenty-eight. And because Valentine's so tall and can look quite glamorous all of a sudden, say if she's wearing makeup, there were times you might have thought that Valentine and not Clover was the grownup.

Still, there was just something so cute about Clover. She made me think of a plump little bluebird. Her voice was very high for a grown woman's, and she talked and moved very fast and kind of fluttered around the apartment. She wore these delicate glasses with rhinestones dusting the tips. And blue was her favorite color—she had fluffy blond hair and big blue eyes and it suited her. The day we met her she was wearing a pale blue dress with breezy bell-shaped sleeves.

We explained to her that in San Francisco, the weather is pretty much the same all year long. We live in blue jeans and T-shirts and Converse sneakers. But even after we told her all that she asked: "But don't you have summer wardrobes?"

I thought the word *wardrobe* sounded very grand, like say you were packing a steamer trunk for a transatlantic crossing.

She continued, "You know, Theo doesn't like trousers."

"*Trousers?*" said Valentine.

Was this an East Coast word or something? We had never heard anybody use it.

"Pants," Clover said, almost spitting the word. "Women in pants."

"Oh."

We pondered the marvelous complexity of a world in which there were such elaborate rules. We had never before dreamed of such things!

Val pointed out, "But that's so old-fashioned of her!"

"Exactly," Clover said calmly, as if the phrase *old-fashioned* was a compliment, which I don't think is what Valentine meant it to be. "She doesn't like trousers on women, or short skirts either. So, when she comes to New York in August, you'll have to be dressed appropriately."

"What's appropriately?" I asked.

"Oh. Well, Aunt Theo says that one should dress to have a swing in one's step and to be ready for Italy. You know, as if you were dressing for an Italian lover."

There was that word again! Lover. It was thrilling, if also a little embarrassing. *Perish. Lover.* Just imagine having the opportunity to use the two of them in the same sentence!

Valentine got straight to the point and asked Clover: "Have you ever had one?"

"What?"

"An Italian lover."

Clover laughed and said, "There's time to ask me all that later. Come on, you two, you'd better unpack. Here, let me show you to your bedroom."

On the way there, we took the time now to look around the apartment. The first thing I noticed was that it was done up in all of these crazy, rich colors. There were autumn-leaf yellow walls in the kitchen and sapphire-blue walls in the living room. Books everywhere. *Old* books. Penguin paperbacks with orange and green spines, big art books, fashion books, you name it. Paintings, mostly of voluptuous shell-colored nudes.

"You know what all these colors kind of remind me of," I said. "Matisse."

Valentine, as if sensing this, said, "Oh, Franny, stop showing off! We're not in school anymore."

"Look!" I pointed at a book on the coffee table, ignoring Val's comment. The cover said: *Made in Paris* by Theodora Bell.

When I picked it up and looked at the jacket, I realized that it was a portrait of the great Theo herself, photographed in profile and wearing a strapless, feathered black ball gown and pair of long lilac gloves. I turned to Clover and asked her:

"Did Aunt Theo really write this? That's so cool. I had no idea."

"Yes," said Clover. "When she was very young. Younger than me, even, I think."

We would be sleeping in the bedroom downstairs. It had dusty coral walls and two twin beds with brass headboards. The sheets and pillows were mismatched, but in a way, I thought, that looked better than matched—like Aunt Theo couldn't be bothered to try that hard. Clover left us to unpack alone, which I thought was nice of her, since of course we had all kinds of things we wanted to talk about right now.

"I get the bed by the window!" exclaimed Val, sitting down on it and sighing. Then she tapped the mattress and said, "Not too comfy a bed actually. And to think I thought Aunt Theo was *loaded*. Actually to tell you the truth this place isn't as fancy as I thought it would be. What do you think, Franny?"

"I love it," I said immediately and rather protectively. But I saw that Val had a point. There was no television, and the kitchen with the dusty black-and-white diamond floors hadn't been remodeled in forever. I started to get the impression that Aunt Theo wasn't big on modern conveniences of any kind.

"Oh my God, I am just dying to read Aunt Theo's novel. Aren't you?"

"Yeah, later maybe," said Valentine, though she's not as big on reading novels as I am, to tell you the truth. "I'm dying of thirst after that flight and I want something sweet ASAP. Lemonade or, I know, let's go get raspberry lime rickeys!" That was our favorite drink back in San Francisco.

"But where will we be able to find them?" I asked her.

"Oh, Franny!" Valentine flashed me her Big Sister look. "It's New York City. You can find anything here."

"Okay, but let's unpack first."

Just as I said this, we heard a knock on the door. It was Clover, saying the magic words: "Girls, would you like to go shopping?"

3

Uncommon Cottons

Clover walked like a real New Yorker, elbows out and eyes straight ahead. When she went outside, she took off her glasses with the rhinestones and put on a pair of huge vanilla-colored sunglasses.

"I got them with Theo in Paris," she said by way of explanation. Then, to Valentine, "You were born there, weren't you?"

"Yes," said Valentine, with a little bit of pride in her voice that I knew her well enough to recognize.

Clover changed the subject by asking us: "Don't you two have sunglasses?"

We shook our heads.

"Oh, I forgot, San Francisco! Those wonderful dreamy fogs rolling in. I love it, it feels so good on my skin. But in New York in the summer, you'll want to get sunglasses. That will be fun, picking sunglasses out."

I was glad that somebody had finally said something good about San Francisco. I felt at such a disadvantage, having been born in California and not Paris, like Val. Or even just the East Coast, where Clover was from and which was obviously superior to the West, or why would Aunt Theo have taken such a strong stand against ever coming to visit us?

But I'd always had this feeling about the East. We had been in New York City one time before when Valentine was eleven and I was eight and the San Francisco Girls Chorus got to perform at Alice Tully Hall, which is part of Lincoln Center. Dad's big on music and still talks about it: *My daughters performed at Alice Tully Hall.*

So we performed at Alice Tully Hall and went to tea at the Plaza and had our pictures taken in front of the portrait of Eloise and went on a pony ride in Central Park. We went to the MoMA and the Met and the Museum of Natural History. We both made up our minds that one day we'd come here again.

You know what I noticed right away when we got here? New York has the most beautiful light. San Francisco is beautiful just generally but New York has this light—it just has this *richness*. It has different dimensions. By now it was going on 6:00 p.m., the heat lifting a bit, and we walked down one of the side streets with all the marvelous old brownstones in all the different shades of brick: red, pink, beige. We don't have much brick like that in San Francisco.

"Oh, this way," said Clover, and we followed her down another one of the side streets till we got to this cool vintage store.

"Oh," Valentine and I swooned, gazing at a full-skirted, fluffy orange dress in the window.

"You could pull off that color," said Clover to Valentine but not, I couldn't help but notice, to me.

We went inside and exclaimed over stiff crinolines, bunny-soft cashmeres, tiny beaded purses.

The lady behind the counter started talking to Clover. She was positively ancient but cool-looking. Her eyelids were all sultry with black liner and she was wearing this black linen sort of sheath dress with coils of turquoise on both her wrists. They looked like underwater creatures, those bracelets, like they might spring to life and bite you.

I eavesdropped on their conversation, catching certain parts.

"But whatever became of the historian?"

"It didn't work out."

"Who broke it off?"

"*He* did."

"Clover," the woman said, "are you trying to tell me you don't have a lover at the moment?"

Clover laughed lightly and said, "Afraid so."

"But, my dear, that's all wrong. I'm seventy-five and I have two."

Lover. That word was in the air, here in the Village, this summer.

Valentine was leafing through an old *Mademoiselle* magazine from July 1948 and lazily reading aloud from the captions on the photo shoots: "The Ultra Violets," "British Imports," "Uncommon Cottons . . ."

Clover said to us, "Girls, this is Joan. Joan, this is Franny and Valentine. They're visiting from San Francisco."

"San Francisco!" said Joan. "I used to work at City Lights. I mean, way back when it started."

Dad was always trying to educate us about local history, and so we did know a little bit about City Lights Bookstore and the Beats. We made conversation about that, and then Joan picked out some clothing for us.

Here is what she chose.

For Valentine: a Mexican circle skirt from the 1950s, heavy green cotton scattered with faint gold gems that jangled a bit whenever she moved.

"See, you can just throw that on with a camisole, and it will look a little more modern," said Clover. "And please don't ever say *tank top*. Say *camisole*: *camisole* is a lovely word. I despair of the words *tank top*."

Valentine did a twirl so we could hear the gems stir again.

"She's a beauty," said Joan to Clover approvingly, and I tried my best not to be jealous. But then Valentine tugged at the waistband of the skirt as though she was just itching to get out of it and said, "No thanks. It's just not for me. It's so heavy . . . and *long*."

She had a point: girls our age almost never wore long skirts anymore. The shorter the better was all the rage, and Val was always disappointed that Mom never let us go out of the house in *really* short ones.

"Well, of course the cotton is heavy," said Joan, bristling. "It's beautiful quality. Young people these days are just used to everything being thin and cheap, you wear it one season and throw it away. Why, that skirt is over fifty years old!"

"Exactly," said Valentine, before slipping back into the dressing room to take it off. I knew that if Mom had been with us, she would have said *Valentine* in that tone of voice to let her know she was being rude. Clover had just met us, so she couldn't get away with scolding her.

I turned out to be a better customer than Valentine. Here is what Joan chose for me: a navy-blue 1960s shift dress with a white Peter Pan collar. I thought at first it looked too babyish, but then

Clover said, "Not at all! On the contrary, it's very sophisticated. And *très française*. Did you ever see *The Umbrellas of Cherbourg?*"

Did we ever see *The Umbrellas of Cherbourg?*

"Oh God," said Valentine, "have we ever! Mom used to make us sing from it all the time!"

"They're singers," Clover explained to Joan. "Classically trained."

"I'll call it my Catherine Deneuve dress," I said, picturing myself wearing a big white bow in my hair like she does in the movie, but more than that, much more than that, picturing myself wearing my new dress and *being in love*. Then my imagination ran off with me. It rains a lot in San Francisco too, you know, just like in the movie. Say I got a trench coat. Say I had a boyfriend. We could wander the hilly streets arm in arm, the rain coming down. We could sing:

> *If it takes forever I will wait for you*
> *For a thousand summers I will wait for you . . .*

And so on and so on, till we got to the end of the song.

Valentine and I decided to get both outfits, even though at first Val had said her skirt was too old-fashioned. Mom and Dad had given us a certain amount of money to spend on shopping in New York, and we thought that these seemed original and worthwhile. Then after Joan had rung up our purchases Clover stopped to look at a soft, woven honey-colored purse with tortoiseshell handles. The woven fabric was something that Clover called "raffia." Joan said it was from the fifties. I didn't quite "get" it, but Clover assured us it was very chic and "ready for Italy" and bought it immediately.

Once we got up to the register, I noticed that Val was trying on scarves. She was tying them softly around her hair, around the beautiful copper curls I wished were mine. When she finished with one scarf, she put it back and picked up another—the last one she picked up was this brilliant shade of green. Back at home, I couldn't recall Val ever wearing that color, but now that I saw her in it, I knew that shade belonged to her alone and that I'd never ever try to wear it myself. Clover and Joan saw it too, and then they did something I thought was strange—they sighed. The way Mom sighs when she remembers Paris. As if they too were remembering something.

"That has to be yours, Valentine," said Clover.

And then I heard Val asking, rudely and rather randomly I thought: "Where does Theo get all her money?"

Clover shrugged and said, "Oh, *that*. Her family made it way, way back. Mills or something."

After we left the store and were walking down the street again, I looked down at my feet and came back to reality. I was wearing a pair of dingy black flip-flops. Valentine was wearing purple ones. Clover had on a pair of white patent-leather sandals, and her toes were painted this luscious peach color.

I made up my mind then and there. We'd have to get new shoes to go with our new clothes. And we'd have to get our toenails painted.

"What's that color?" I asked Clover. "I mean, the one on your toes?"

"Oh, that," said Clover, looking down at her toes with a sly little smile. "Italian Love Affair."

The Secret Roof-Deck

$\mathcal{I}$t was Clover who got the idea to give Aunt Theo a party on August 14, the night she was supposed to arrive back in New York.

"A birthday party?" asked Valentine. "Old people don't always like to be reminded of their birthdays, you know."

"Never you mind about old people," said Clover. "And anyway, her birthday's in October, not August."

"So it's more like a welcome back party then," I said, trying to sound more knowledgeable about these things than Valentine.

"Yes, I suppose so," said Clover. "Although you know what kind of party Aunt Theo used to have when I was your age?"

"What?"

"She called them Getting to Know You parties."

"A *what* party?"

"A Getting to Know You party," Clover repeated. "You see, Aunt Theo used to have these parties where the whole idea was to bring a fascinating stranger. So, I would have to go scampering all over the streets of the Village introducing myself to possible strangers to invite. 'Unknowns,' Aunt Theo called them. At the beginning of the party, we always had this special ritual we did. Aunt Theo would make us all hold hands and sing 'Getting to Know You.' And then after that, the party could begin."

"I wouldn't be caught dead," announced Valentine.

"You wouldn't be caught dead what?" asked Clover, smiling.

"Holding hands *with strangers*. Singing songs *with strangers*."

"Well, I would!" I said, just to be contrary. "I think it sounds—interesting."

"Franny! Mom and Dad raised us not to speak to strangers."

"Well, if you're so big on doing only what Mom and Dad say—"

"Girls! Stop all this quarreling. Never you mind. Anyway, I don't imagine that your parents would much like it if I had you two dragging strangers off the streets, so let's just call this a Welcome Back party, shall we? Whatever we call it, the important thing is to make it a party to remember."

I liked that idea—"a party to remember." I was looking forward to planning it, and most of all, to finally meeting Aunt Theo in person. But then, right from the beginning, I think I was more interested in the characters of Aunt Theodora and her protégée Clover Leslie than Valentine was. That's how I thought of Theo and Clover—as characters out of an old-fashioned novel who had suddenly appeared in our lives, making everything somehow more colorful and fascinating than before. Anyway, here are some things I learned about Clover Leslie:

1. She was an orphan. When she was growing up in Boston, Aunt Theo was her guardian.

"For how long?" Valentine asked.

"Forever," said Clover, and we didn't ask her any more

questions about that, though of course we wanted to know how her parents had died or if they'd gone missing or what. Our curiosity was only natural, the same way it's only natural that Valentine wants to know who her real father is.

2. Clover was a sculptress. She had gone to Bennington, which is a tiny school on a hill in Vermont that is famous for artists and writers and modern dancers. After school, she got a studio in the Village and had had some shows and sold her pieces to very high-end stores on the Upper East Side. Her work, she said, was more uptown than downtown because her sensibility (that was a new word; I filed it away) was old-fashioned. She was a classicist, she said: another new word. There were a couple of her sculptures at Aunt Theo's apartment and she showed them to us. They were tiny and of mysterious sea creatures; the white porcelain was touched with pale blue, her favorite color.

"Do you have a thing about the ocean?" asked Valentine.

"Absolutely," said Clover.

"Do you ever do anything else? Like, do you ever do nudes?"

"Val!" I exclaimed, embarrassed.

But Clover only said casually, "Sure. All the time."

"Male nudes?"

"Sure, why not?"

"Do you have male models? Like, at your studio?"

"Sometimes."

"You do? Oh my God. Are they cute?"

"*Val!*"

"Of course. Why would I sculpt them if they weren't?" said Clover, and laughed. Clover laughed a lot but we never felt that she was laughing *at us*, the way you do with some grownups.

When Clover wasn't wearing blue, she wore pale pink. Every so often, gray. Blond colors. But mostly she wore blue. Blue cotton dresses, blue gingham artist smocks, sheer blue nighties, lacy blue bras and underpants: I know, because she always hand-washed them.

She hand-washed almost all of her clothing, actually. We thought that was funny at first. She'd swish around the apartment wringing her clothing out in a bucket full of lavender-scented soapsuds. Actually it was a white-painted champagne bucket that she told me Aunt Theo had gotten from some hotel in Paris. The paint was chipping now, but it still looked pretty dashing to me. In fact, like a lot of Aunt Theo's things, it almost looked better because it was chipped—because it gave off an air of history. Back home, Valentine and I just tossed everything into the washing machine. This ritual of hand-washing was something new and grownup. It made Clover seem like such a lady.

Rules, Aunt Theo had written to us in a second letter on the same lavender-colored paper as the one before.

Clover, your chaperone, will have a private bedroom and bath. You are not welcome to them, but everything else in the apartment is yours for the summer. Clover is an artist and needs time to herself during the day but most especially in the morning. In the evening she will be game for anything.

The apartment had two floors and Clover slept on the top one. Valentine and I went to sleep every night next to each other on the hard little twin beds with brass headboards. We understood that this was only appropriate at our age, sharing a bedroom together. We were still girls. Clover was a woman.

Other times, when Aunt Theo was in New York, the top floor was her bedroom. Clover only lived there when Aunt Theo was away on her travels. One time, we asked Clover where she lived the rest of the year.

"Out of an orange suitcase," she said, with that light little laugh of hers.

"Why *orange?*" said Valentine. I knew she was wondering that because Clover always wore blue.

"It's Hermès," said Clover, and explained to us that orange was the color of the Hermès brand.

I've noticed this thing about Valentine: she won't let things be. I get it when grownups go silent. And I don't mind filling in the blanks in my head.

But not Valentine. She kept right at it. She said: "Why don't you live here? You could sleep in our room, couldn't you?"

"Girls! You don't understand. Aunt Theo believes in *alone time.*"

The way she believed in skirts but didn't believe in trousers, the way she believed in letters but not e-mail . . . I was trying to keep track of it all so one day I too could understand.

"And then," Clover went on, "if I were here, how would she entertain her gentleman friends?"

The phrase *entertain her gentleman friends* was quite beyond us, especially when we both knew Aunt Theo was well into her sixties by now, and even Valentine stopped pushing it. One couldn't be interested in that side of life then; one simply couldn't.

The next afternoon when Clover was out doing some errands,

Valentine yawned and said, "You know what I'd like to do right now?"

"What?"

"Go upstairs."

I was about to say, "Oh, Val!" But what I ended up saying instead was: "Me too."

We were giggling as we made our way upstairs. The banister was painted this bottle-green color but the paint was chipping. Well, that wasn't unusual: most everything at Aunt Theo's was chipping.

"Do you think that means she's very poor or very rich?" Valentine asked.

"Neither," I said. "It's just her aesthetic."

"*Her aesthetic*? Oh, Jesus. Who are you trying to sound like? Clover?"

"No."

But Valentine had caught me. I *was* trying to sound like Clover, though I hadn't noticed it before she pointed it out.

We went up the green staircase till we got to a landing with the same brown-and-white diamond parquet floor as the lobby of the apartment building. There was a salmon-colored velvet cotton curtain you had to tug at to cross into the bedroom. I liked this odd little space. It made you pause. It made you wonder what the bedroom would be like, rather than you jumping into the bedroom right away. But Valentine pulled at the curtain impatiently and then, all at once, we were standing there.

Aunt Theo's bedroom was painted red but a red that had a lot of dimension to it, a lot of roses and oranges enfolded in it. A mysterious red, something I had never seen before, because I'd always thought of red being kind of obvious. On the floor was an Oriental rug that was all olive greens and golds. And on the bed itself was a leopard-skin blanket, soft and touchable and yet kind of dangerous-looking at the same time.

"Cool," said Valentine, and I knew it was the leopard-skin she was referring to.

As in the rest of the apartment, there were lots of old books and paintings, and the paintings were mostly of nudes.

"Come on," I said. "Let's keep looking. Clover might be back any minute."

We got closer to the bed, where Clover's pet turtle, Carlo, was snuggled up in a fold of the leopard skin. We were surprised at first to see the turtle out of a cage, but looked down only to notice his tiny cage at the foot of the bed.

"Ah," said Valentine, leaning over to stroke him. Then she said, "Hey, I think that one's of Aunt Theo, isn't it?" and pointed to the painting above the bed.

It was yet another nude and showed the tall, willowy lines of a beautiful brunette captured in a pale blue light. What was interesting about the portrait to me was that Aunt Theo was looking straight ahead without apology. Her body was less developed than many of the other nudes, but next to her, they looked like schoolgirls and she looked like a grown woman.

I wondered if I'd ever look like that.

"That picture was painted in Paris," Valentine said.

"How do you know?"

"I just can tell. Paris in the morning. Something about that shade of blue, that light."

A title was written in cursive in the bottom corner of the

painting. The title was: *L'heure de la lavande*, "The Lavender Hour." I read it out loud.

"Can you imagine letting someone see you naked?" asked Valentine.

"Oh my God, no. Can *you*?"

What she said surprised me: "Sometimes." And I saw that this must be one of the differences between being fourteen and being seventeen. Because I couldn't imagine letting someone see me naked: I blushed, I almost wanted to throw up, just to think of it.

Then Val opened the door to Clover's private bath, which is where we saw her lacy blue bra and undies dripping over the side of the claw-foot tub.

"I'm so going to wear sexy lingerie as soon as I have a guy who's going to see it," said Valentine. "But I wouldn't wear blue, I don't think. I'm going to wear black! Black lace and what are those things called, garters. God, I can't wait. Franny, do you think Clover has someone?"

"She told that woman in the shop that she didn't."

Valentine said, "Well, not now, but she has. She has in the past, and I'm going to get her to tell us all about it. I need *information*."

"About what, Val?"

"Sex, dummy."

"Oh."

"I mean," Val went on, "it's New York City, there have to be so many men around! And Mom and Dad aren't here to bug me, and another thing: I can totally pull anything over Clover."

"*Val*. Clover's our chaperone."

"Whatever, she's shorter than both of us! I know what we've

got to do, Franny. We've got to get dressed up and hit the town and meet some men."

I didn't want to let on in front of Val, but the truth was, the whole idea kind of embarrassed me. I got shy even just talking to boys at school.

"Enough of that, Val," I said. "Come on, let's look around up here before Clover gets back."

The bathroom was all white, or rather antique white, with chipping white-painted furniture and more of those brown-and-white diamond parquet floors. I had never seen so many beauty products in one bathroom and all with the most delicate hand-printed wrappings and labels. White Almond Talcum Powder. Hyacinth & Bluebell Bubble Bath. Bars of French soap: *Mielle, Violette, Pepins de Raisins, Fleur d'Orange.*

We were so busy looking at the beauty products that it took us a while to notice that there were French doors leading outside.

"Does Clover have her own balcony?" said Valentine. *"Jealous."*

By now, Carlo had gotten off the bed and was following us, waddling across the parquet floor.

"Oh, Carlo," I said, and scooped his silky green body into the palm of my hand while Valentine twisted the doorknob.

And then we were outside. It wasn't a balcony, it was a whole roof-deck, *a secret roof-deck.*

"Oh my God," said Valentine, "Clover was keeping this from us? I *hate* her."

"Quiet. She might be back at any minute."

I haven't been to Italy yet, but that's what this roof-deck felt like to me—like being in Italy. Having a—what was the name of

Clover's toenail polish again?—*Italian Love Affair*. There were all these fancy terra-cotta pots that held geraniums and lavender and even lemons, these tiny lemons with thin crinkly skins, not like the big beautiful juicy ones we have in California. But still! Lemons. Lemons growing on a roof-deck, here in New York City! The floor of the roof-deck was covered in green-and-white tiles, some of which were missing so you had to be careful where you stepped. And there was a blue-greenish wrought-iron table with a couple of matching chairs. On the table, an espresso cup with the remains of Clover's morning coffee, and a vase of dying yellow roses.

At the foot of the table was a sculpture of a small blue swan. Its feet were ringed by different size seashells. I wondered if that was one of Clover's sculptures.

"Oh my God," said Valentine, "a sofa! *Sweet.*"

I would have called it a love seat, though if I had, Valentine would have said: "Who are you trying to sound like? Clover?" So I didn't. Anyway, it was under a canopy of white muslin and it was green, green velvet. Imagine, just imagine it, *lying on a velvet sofa* in the middle of New York City.

No, not in the middle of New York City, on top of New York City! Here we were, on the seventeenth floor of this huge apartment building.

"Let's check out the view," I said, and so we did, leaning over the railing as far and as long as we could, taking in the blue and green and red brick sweep of the city, how beautiful it was and all ours, ours to explore.

"Oh my God, look!" exclaimed Val, pointing.

"What?"

"That couple is totally making out!"

"Where?" After I said it, I was embarrassed by the quickening of my voice. I shouldn't have given away my excitement quite so easily.

"There, on that roof-deck, the one with the geraniums, the pink geraniums, see."

I looked, searching for the pink of the geraniums, and finally found it. Val was right: a couple was lying in each other's arms and kissing on a blue deck chair. It was a wonderful artificial blue, the blue of a swimming pool, and the two of them looked so happy on this summer afternoon. I noticed a pitcher of pink lemonade on the table next to them and pointed this out to Val.

"You're not supposed to be paying attention to pink lemonade, Franny," she said. "You're supposed to be paying attention to what they're *doing.*"

"But they're just—kissing."

"Kissing goes other places," said Val darkly.

5

Lilac Gloves

*B*efore we went to New York, Dad gave us this speech about the importance of making the most of our time in the city. Go see the Statue of Liberty, he said. Make sure you get to Rockefeller Center. Don't miss the Whitney. It's time you learned something about modern art. How about we get you girls tickets to a Broadway show? He was disappointed that the Metropolitan Opera wasn't in town for the summer or he would have loved getting us tickets.

"Edward," said Mom. "Don't worry about it so much. I want you girls to have a wonderful time in the city and just *be*."

And then she smiled at us, a little sadly, I thought at the time.

It turned out that Valentine enjoyed being a tourist much better than I did. She wanted to do all the things Dad said we should do, and in those first few weeks I went with her, and we had fun.

I think Mom and Dad had this idea that Clover would take us on activities all around the city. After all, Theo had described her as our "chaperone," and that sounded like what a chaperone was supposed to do with her young charges. But actually Clover wasn't big on activities, or not on pre-planned ones anyway. We learned that there were a couple of reasons for this. One was that during the daytime, as Theo had explained to us in her letter, Clover was supposed to be working in her studio. The other reason was that Theo—and therefore Clover herself—didn't *do* activities.

Clover explained this to us by saying:

"The first time I went to Paris, I think I must have been, oh, ten years old. As soon as we got there, the first thing Theo did was assign us code names for the visit. We needed French names, see. So she named herself Jacqueline and *me* Celeste. And then I'll never forget her saying to me, 'Don't think we're going to the Eiffel Tower, young lady. Don't think we're going to see the Notre Dame Cathedral. Here's what I like to do when I travel, see. I like to pretend that I live in the place I'm going. I find a favorite café to have my coffee in the morning and once you have that, the rest just falls into place.' "

Clover shrugged her shoulders and added, "And you know something? She was right. The rest *did* just fall into place."

I think the point of this conversation was lost on Valentine, but it made quite an impression on me. Back home, I'd often felt overscheduled what with homework, Girls Chorus, sleepovers, and so on, and I loved the idea of a whole, empty summer stretching before me. When I was little, Mom called me her "little dreamer" because I was quite happy to be left alone with my dolls and make up stories and do as I pleased. Whereas Valentine was always springing up with her red curls and demanding to "do" something.

Now in New York it was no different. Here is what Val said about Clover, muttering under her breath: "Some chaperone."

"I like her," I said. "I think she's lovely."

"Lovely." Val imitated my voice, and I couldn't help but notice how young she made me sound. "You'd think *a chaperone* could get something going for us, instead of being at her studio all day. Why—I'm bored. I've never been so bored in all my life!"

The way Valentine said the word *bored,* curling her lips, was almost convincing, but only almost. I knew she was just trying to get a reaction out of me.

"You know something else?" she went on. "She never takes us anywhere *new*, do you notice that? Everywhere we go has been around for, like, ever and ever." She groaned.

"Well—she learned everything she knows from Aunt Theo . . ."

"Who's an *old lady*. That's what I'm saying! When we get back home, I want to be able to tell my friends we did things that were *cool*." For a second, Val's face went very dark and serious, just for effect. Then it brightened right up again. "Let's—go to Rockefeller Center!" she said. "Come on, let's go right now."

"No thanks, Val."

"But, Franny, I'm bored, I'm so bored I could—"

"I know, but Rockefeller Center's just not my thing," I said. I liked how disdainful it sounded. *Just not my thing.*

"Oh please," said Valentine. "Don't forget, Franny, you're younger than me."

So while Valentine was off swanning about Rockefeller Center, I stayed home and did something I had been meaning to do ever since we got to New York, which was read Theo's novel, *Made in Paris.* I went and lay on my twin bed and read the whole thing in one afternoon.

Here is what I could make of it.

There's this heroine, Angelica Randall, not to be called under any circumstances Angie. She's from this big family in Boston that has its own island, called Cranberry Cliff, somewhere around the Cape Cod area. Angelica's brothers and sisters and cousins are always off playing tennis and drinking gin and tonics. Or sometimes they drink martinis.

Angelica goes to this stuffy all-girls school, called Winters, with an old-maid headmistress, Miss Shattuck, who doesn't approve when Angelica refuses to play volleyball and tries to get other girls to refuse too. You're warned, Angelica, Miss Shattuck tells her. Then Angelica invites an eighteen-year-old sailor, Tony, to a school dance. (She doesn't call it a "prom.") So then Miss Shattuck expels her from Winters, which is a big disgrace because the women in her family have gone to Winters *forever*. Her father sends her to a boarding school in Virginia, which she says is "a very boring, very green state where all the girls are just crazy about horses. I am not crazy about horses."

I guess getting expelled from Winters wasn't too terrible, because she gets into Radcliffe anyway. And that's where she starts having a ton of boyfriends. But a lot of Harvard guys are boring, and good, she says, for only one thing. But then things get serious with a dark-eyed poet named Clay Claverly, whose last name is the name of a building at Harvard, so "even Mummy and Daddy will approve of him." Angelica steals his black turtlenecks and wears them around campus with her plaid skirts, and she and Clay are always smoking and kissing in public, at a hangout called the Blue Parrot.

But then Angelica gets pregnant. I was thinking they'd get married they were so in love, but you don't have a novel unless something goes wrong. So before you know it they've fallen out of love, and Angelica doesn't want to have a baby anyway. She gets *a procedure*, which of course is an abortion.

Then she goes to Paris.

One day, she's just sitting in a café when a man asks her if she's ever done any modeling. She says no, but she's up for anything. And she is: she goes to a wild party at a chateau in the countryside. She cross-dresses: "Turns out I look just dashing in a tux." But then one day when the chestnut trees are shedding and winter is coming, she gets a letter from her father's lawyer saying: Come back to Boston or I won't give you any more money.

You don't know, when the book ends, whether Angelica will go back to Boston or stay in Paris or what. You just know that she's had all these experiences and *lived*, the way Val said we were going to "live" this summer in New York.

When Val got home, I gave her the novel, figuring she'd want to read it. But Val only rolled her eyes and said: "But, Franny, you just told me most of the plot yourself! And anyway—I don't know, Aunt Theodora is so old!" She glanced at the photograph of her on the cover, wearing those long lilac gloves. She read aloud from the back flap: " 'Theodora Bell is a Radcliffe graduate and former model. *Made in Paris* is her first novel.' Hmm. Do you think she was ever really young?"

"Well of course, Val!" I exclaimed. "Just look at the picture."

"Well. Put it another way. Do you think *we'll* ever be really old?"

That evening, Clover took us to dinner at the cute little Italian restaurant down the street, and I asked her something I had been wondering about more and more: "What is Aunt Theo doing in Germany?"

Clover usually answers things quickly, but this time she didn't.

"I don't think," said Clover, "that she would think that was a very polite question for you to ask."

We went back to eating our spaghetti carbonara. That's spaghetti with eggs and bacon, and is that combination ever delicious. Then Clover said to the waiter, "Please, another glass of wine," and we were left wondering just what it might be that she was trying to hide.

6

Nudes

Sometimes we liked to go and have picnics right across the street in Washington Square Park. That was Clover's suggestion, and she made a special point of getting some of our favorite foods— after asking us to list them—so that we could pack the picnic ourselves and not spend money on going out to lunch every single day. Also, Val and I liked playing around in the kitchen every once in a while. What we did is: spread ricotta and figs and some honey on brown bread. If we had any figs left over after we made our sandwiches, we took those to nibble on; you can never have too many figs. Then, we packed those tiny brown bottles of Italian soda called Sanpellegrino Chinotto, more bitter than American soft drinks and absolutely delicious. Back home Mom and Dad didn't like us to have any soda, even if it's Italian. But we talked Clover into getting us a pack of it anyway. After all, it wouldn't be a summer away from home if we weren't allowed to get away with at least a little something that we wouldn't ordinarily.

One day we were in the park eating our picnic when I asked Val: "Aren't you ever going to read Aunt Theo's novel?"

"Hmm, probably not," she said.

"But aren't you even curious?"

Val appeared to consider this, selecting a fig.

"These aren't quite ripe yet, I don't think. It's still too early in the summer." Then: "Curious, curious? Am I even curious? I guess I'd have to say: not really, Franny."

"But *I* am."

"Well, you always were more of a reader than me, Mom says."

"Yes," I agreed. "It's like ever since I read Aunt Theo's novel I'm under this spell. It's like I'm living in my head not right here"—I tapped the grass where we were sitting—"not right here in New York City with you, but somewhere else, somewhere you couldn't even point to on a map, not even if you tried. It's like I'm living in a dorm room at Radcliffe in the 1960s, say, or a café in Paris . . ."

"Weird," was all that Valentine said.

"I know, right?"

"Totally!" We giggled.

"Aren't you even curious to meet Aunt Theo when she comes in August, though?"

"Oh, yeah, sure, I want to see what the big deal is. Also, we're having a party. There might be cute boys there."

"Um, I think there will be more like older men."

"I'm curious about them too, actually."

"*Valentine.*"

"So what?"

"You're boy-crazy!"

"I'm seventeen," said Val, as if that explained everything, and who knows? Maybe it did.

Later on that same night, I heard Clover crying. I don't think she knew I saw her, but I did. I tiptoed upstairs to ask her a question and I was standing in the entryway just behind the salmon-colored velvet curtain when I heard the sound of tears, not tiny trickle-trickle tears but rough, broken-sounding ones. So then I turned and went back downstairs.

I told Valentine about it, but she didn't seem too upset. She was lounging on the bed in her underwear and eating a nectarine, her long copper curls falling peek-a-boo style over half of her face.

She shrugged and said, "Maybe she just has her period."

"*Val!*"

That's the kind of thing boys are supposed to say, not your older sister.

"Well, I feel like hell when I have mine. Ugh, none of my jeans fit me, and all I want to do is eat chocolate *bad*. Nutella! That's what I crave. Nutella."

The truth was, I had to admit that she had a point. I'd just gotten my period last year and I absolutely hated it. But I didn't want to discuss it with her, or with anyone else for that matter.

So I said: "I don't think so. I think there's something a little sad about Clover, don't you? As if—as if life hadn't worked out the way she'd hoped."

"Who *does* it work out for?" said Valentine, lazing around and, at this moment, absolutely gorgeous.

Sometimes I wished Valentine wasn't quite so comfortable in her underwear. Back in San Francisco, we both went to bed in old T-shirts and pajama bottoms, and when we were getting undressed we'd be pretty modest. We'd make a point of turning around when we had our tops off, or we'd hold our T-shirts up to our boobs so no one could see. I still did that. It was only polite.

But Val, well, it's like this summer she gets in and she can't get undressed fast enough. I know that it's hotter here, but *still*. The way Valentine peels off her clothing, it's like she's all damp and bursting. And then when she has to get dressed again to go outside, she acts annoyed about it, like putting on clothes is this big personal inconvenience.

"Maybe it's because she's not married."

"Who?"

"Clover, silly."

"Oh."

"Wouldn't you want to be married if you were that old?"

"You were the one who said twenty-eight's not that old."

"Not to be married it is."

"But Mom didn't get married until she was thirty-one, right? And then she had me."

"Uh-huh."

"But when you were born, she was—what? Twenty-eight? And—"

"Oh, Franny, stop it!" burst out Val.

"Stop what? What am I doing?"

"You're always doing this. You're always trying to make us talk about *him*."

I knew that she meant her father. But the way she said the word *him* this time was kind of funny—it sounded dismissive and impatient. She sounds like a real *teenager* now, I thought, forgetting that I was a teenager myself.

"We've always talked about him," I said.

"When we were little," said Valentine, as if she were reading my mind. "When we were little, Franny, and we're not that little anymore."

It's true, what Valentine says. She's starting to look like the portraits.

I mean, like the nudes. She's filled out that way and I guess that's why it's like she's bursting.

You know, there's only one nude in the apartment who doesn't look like that. Aunt Theo herself. Aunt Theo in her portrait is all long lines and bones.

I'm five foot seven now and still growing. I don't really have any boobs or hips yet to speak of. So the funny thing is, out of all the bodies in the portraits, the one mine most looks like is Aunt Theodora's.

Sometimes, sometimes when Clover's out on an errand I tiptoe upstairs and gaze at Aunt Theodora's portrait looming over the bed. She stares at me out of the thin blue light of that Parisian morning. I can't wait to ask her who painted it, when I finally meet her in person.

Yesterday a letter came from Aunt Theo, addressed to me. This was out of the ordinary because most of her letters are addressed to Clover, and then Clover reads them aloud to us, skipping certain parts. I had a feeling that those were probably the most interesting parts, but anyway it was nice of her to read aloud from the letters at all.

The letter was addressed to "Miss Frances Lord," in Aunt Theo's unmistakable handwriting on a cinnamon-colored envelope, so I opened it. I didn't even wait until Val got home.

Here is what the letter said.

Dear Frances,

But I think you go by Franny. One of these days you'll have to grow into Frances, which in my view is a name of substance, so why not start growing into it now?

From what Clover tells me about you two girls, you, not Valentine, are the proper one to confide things in.

I'm writing about Clover. I know it was I who told you she needed her alone time, but now I am worried she is growing slack in her capacities as chaperone.

Not that I want you bustling around the city like tourists. I do want you to treat your time in New York like you live there. But:

You ought to have some nights to remember. And so, ask Clover to take you someplace swanky, but for Lord's sake don't make it too trendy. And do, do, do dress up! No trousers.

Report back to me on your progress. I'll be interested to see if a girl of your generation can write a decent letter, but, Frances my dear, I have a feeling you can.

XXX
Theo

Someplace swanky but not too trendy . . . the Plaza, obviously. We could go there for cocktails! Well, Clover could get a cocktail, and we could get Shirley Temples or something. I suggested this to Clover. She groaned and said:

"Oh, Franny! You're sweet to think of it, but the Plaza's not like it was when Eloise lived there, you know. It's just not like that anymore. Why, Donald Trump owns it." She shuddered delicately at the name.

I suddenly felt very young and foolish and not like a New Yorker at all.

But then Clover smiled at me and said, "Oh, don't worry, I know just the place. Let me just make sure we go on a night when Warren's working."

"Where?" I asked.

"Who's Warren?" asked Valentine.

"Warren is an old flame of Theo's."

"Oh," we both said. It figured.

"And the destination?" I asked.

"The destination," said Clover, "is Bemelmans Bar."

7

The Older Man

A couple of nights later, we all got dressed up to go to Bemelmans. Clover said that I could wear my Catherine Deneuve dress, the navy-blue shift with the white Peter Pan collar. I said I thought maybe it wasn't dressy enough but she said: "Oh no, trust me. It's exactly right."

That's a phrase of Clover's. *It's exactly right.* She says it whenever she approves of something. Which makes you think that in her world a lot of other things must go under the heading: *exactly wrong.* Here is what she told us in a nutshell about the world today: "We are hardly living in the golden age."

Meanwhile, Valentine said, "But I don't have anything fancy! We just wear jeans or leggings in San Francisco. It's true what they say about the East Coast. Everyone here is so uptight!"

Clover took a good long look at her and said, "You know, I think we're about the same measurements, you're just so much taller. You already have quite the figure actually. If you don't mind something being short on you, I bet I can find you something of mine."

A little while later, she came back with a backless sea-green sheath dress in a light, breezy silk. It looked like something to have cocktails in in an old movie. But Valentine said, "No back, that's weird. I wish it were low-cut."

Clover said, "Trust me, this way it's much more subtle."

"Subtle?" echoed Valentine. "But, Clover, I don't want to be subtle."

Clover laughed and said, "No, at your age, I don't suppose you would," and ended up letting Valentine get away with borrowing a pair of alligator pumps of Theo's ("Don't tell") and putting on gobs of dark green eyeliner. Then she said, "Put up your hair. No, no, not straight back. Up, up in a twist. Then pull some of the curls out in front. That's it, you've got it."

The dress was very short and very tight on Valentine and she looked absolutely fantastic and she knew it.

I thought how crummy it was to be fourteen years old and have to look all *jeune fille* in a Peter Pan collar and my pale pink ballet flats, when my sister was trotting around in a pair of the great Theodora Bell's alligator pumps.

Clover, as if sensing this, said, "You look very pretty tonight, Franny, and very Parisian."

"Thanks, Clover."

"Okay, you two! Now it's time for me to go get dressed."

When Clover came downstairs again, she looked completely different. Gone was the cute little bluebird whose soft blond hair was often messy. She had on a cool black linen sheath. Her lashes were very black and her lips were very pale pink, almost white, and her hair was smoothed back into a bun at the nape of her neck. She looked grown up and rather serious. But glamorous. Definitely glamorous.

Then she threw a beautiful soft pink-and-red shawl over her

shoulders, which made her look more like an artist, which she was.

"Aunt Theo got this for me once, in Budapest."

"Oh, Clover!" I said, marveling at her transformation, at how many women one woman can be.

She smiled and said, "Don't forget. I *am* your chaperone."

Bemelmans Bar was located all the way on the Upper East Side at the Carlyle, which is this *very* swanky hotel. As soon as we went inside the bar, I figured out why it's called "Bemelmans"—because that's the last name of the guy who did the *Madeline* books and his drawings are all over the walls. Valentine figured it out too.

"Cool," she said, sounding for once not like she was trying to be seventeen and unimpressed with everything. It was like there were stars in her eyes when she exclaimed: "Madeline!"

Mom used to read us those books at bedtime when we were little, and then later on when we started learning French they were some of the first things we read in the language. So we felt that we knew Madeline like she was a real person, and it was exciting to be here at Bemelmans Bar with the mural of all these darling bunnies wearing green jackets and sitting under peppermint-striped umbrellas.

"See how delicate and how intimate Bemelmans's hand is," said Clover, pointing. "I love how the images aren't perfect, you know. You can imagine his hand kind of wavering over some of them."

We sat down in the most comfortable seats ever. They were made out of this red velvet that was unlike any other velvet I had ever known. The touch was just that much richer.

"Oh my God, I could *sleep* here," said Valentine.

"Well, before you nod off," said Clover, "which waiter do you think is the cutest?"

"That one." Valentine pointed at a young, broad-shouldered blond busboy who I could just tell was totally conceited. So then I pointed to an older gentleman behind the bar and said, "No, that one."

I wasn't kidding. There was something about him that had caught my eye. For one thing, he was remarkably tall, well over six feet. Something about his height, as well as the important way he carried himself, made him appear theatrical, as though he were a bartender in a play, just waiting for his cue. He was going salt-and-pepper now, but I knew that in the past he'd been just as tall, dark, and handsome as could be. His hazel eyes had laughter in them. I thought: I bet *he* could tell you stories.

Valentine said, "Oh no, Franny. He's *old*. My waiter is much cuter."

But Clover said, "Well done, Franny. That's Warren."

She waved to him, and he did the most exciting thing—he bowed.

Valentine and I giggled. We were hardly used to men bowing, these days.

Clover said, "Warren's an actor."

Aha! So I had been onto something. Valentine would never have guessed that.

Our waiter came over to the table, and Clover ordered something called a Lillet Blonde.

"It matches your hair?" asked Valentine, dazzled.

"Well, sort of," said Clover. "It's pale."

Then she ordered food for us to share: some Bemelmans mini

burgers, smoked salmon on toast points, shrimp cocktail, and Caesar salad with lobster.

"The thing is, we've had all of that stuff before," Valentine complained. "Like, shrimp cocktail and Caesar salad are on restaurant menus *everywhere*."

"No, no," said Clover. "You're missing the point. These dishes are classics and also very chic. You might as well say, oh, I don't want another little black dress, I already have a black dress. But you can never have too many little black dresses. Also! Don't worry, girls. We can order really fancy desserts!"

That cheered Val up, as she always thought that dessert was the most important part of any meal.

So then Clover got her Lillet Blonde, which was pale and served in a tiny glass, and we got Shirley Temples. Valentine wasn't going to get one at first because she didn't want to look childish, and I could tell she was jealous that Clover got to look at the cocktail list. But I said, "Come on, Val, you know you like them," and you know what? I was right. She slurped hers up as soon as she got it.

"I remember how at your age," said Clover, "I used to be so big on sugar. There was nothing I wouldn't do for a chocolate bar. Those were the days."

"You don't eat sugar anymore?" I asked her.

"Not like that," she said sadly, "not like that."

"What, do you have to watch your weight?" asked Valentine. I thought that was unkind of her, and she must have only asked it because she was mad that Clover had made her feel like a child by saying, "I remember how at your age . . ."

"No," said Clover. "It's just that after a certain point, one finds one's cravings change. There start to be—other things . . ."

"What things?" Valentine demanded, determined for Clover not to have any secrets, but then before Clover could answer, our food arrived.

And then later on, before we even had a chance to look at the dessert menu, the most magical thing happened. *They sent us dessert.* Without us even asking! The desserts just appeared, delivered by, of all people, the young blond busboy Val had admired at the beginning of the evening.

And then, he bowed! Just as Warren had bowed behind the bar.

And then, he actually said: "Ladies, with our compliments."

The desserts were bittersweet chocolate cake and crème brûlée, and they were everything we'd ever dreamed of.

"A palate cleanser, I think, Warren," said Clover after we had finished the desserts and were thoroughly stuffed and Warren finally had come away from the bar to sit down with us and visit. "Do you still have that delicious strawberry ice? That used to be my favorite."

"Of course." He looked around the dining room and caught the eye of the blond busboy. "Alex," he said. "For the young ladies, how about some strawberry ice?"

Now, I liked Warren, and up close I still did think he was very handsome even though he was old. But here's the thing: he kept on paying attention to Valentine. I know she looked so grown up what with Clover's green backless dress and Aunt Theo's pumps, but still. She's only seventeen and not very mature, not really, if you want to ask me, and I would be the one to know.

"I am an actor," Warren announced. "And you," he said to Valentine, "are an actress."

Valentine said, "A singer actually."

"Torch songs," he said. "Am I right? You must sing torch songs. Broken hearts, lost loves, all that . . ."

"They sing in the Girls Chorus of San Francisco," said Clover, looking very amused. "*And* they go to French school."

"Charming!" said Warren, giving Valentine's hand a little squeeze. "Absolutely charming."

Now she couldn't look bored: no way could she pull that off. Her eyes under their gobs of dark green liner got very wide, and I knew she'd be bragging about tonight *for weeks.*

Our ices came, and Clover said, "Tell them a story, Warren. They'll like that. Tell them the story of how you met Theo."

Here is the story that Warren told us while we were eating our ices.

"It was in Harvard Square in the seventies. I had just moved to Boston and I was very young, oh, twenty-two, twenty-three. Theo was older. She'd graduated from Radcliffe in the mid-sixties and had been living in Paris for a number of years. Modeling and all that. But when she was about thirty, she moved back to Boston for a while, I think it was around the time her father was dying and he wrote her, begging her to come home—"

"It's like something out of *The Ambassadors*," interrupted Clover.

"What's that?" asked Valentine.

"Henry James. Oh, you're probably too young for him. *Daisy Miller*, maybe. Warren, continue."

"I met Theo one autumn day at the Blue Parrot. Which was a wonderful place that like a lot of places isn't there anymore. Anyway—I used to be a waiter there. At the Blue Parrot. By the way, being a bartender is totally different from being a waiter: whole other set of skills. It relies on more of a human dimension.

Back then I was waiting tables at the Blue Parrot, and one night Theo and her cousin Honor come in wearing these new dresses they had around that time, they were all the rage, this Swedish brand called Marimekko."

"Finnish actually," interrupted Clover.

"Whatever. Point is, pow! A lot of girls, they couldn't pull off those dresses. They're real short and this kind of square cut with all these crazy graphic patterns. They're really *alive*, you know? They just bring back that whole time to me. I remember that the one Theo had on that day was black and white actually, and that just shows you. She didn't need to wear a bright color to just pop. Her cousin didn't look too shabby either. She went on to become this famous modern dancer here in New York, Honor Linden, but Theo was the one who took my heart, right then and there, and she never gave it back.

"Now, a good waiter is not supposed to eavesdrop. But: I was not a good waiter. Never was. Bartending's the thing with me. So I couldn't help eavesdropping on Theo and Honor, and what I figured out was that Theo had left behind some guy in Paris and now it was all over and Daddy didn't understand, he'd been the love of her life. Who was this guy in Paris? I never knew. When I had to bring them the check, it was like my heart was breaking. I couldn't bear the thought of never seeing her again. Well, lucky for me, I *was* pretty good-looking in those days, I don't mind telling you, and I didn't have too bad a time with the ladies. So I remember that after they had paid I put my hand out and I said, 'My name is Warren,' and I asked for her number.

"She said, 'What's your last name, Warren? Honor here and I believe in using one's last name when introducing one's self.'

" 'Vittadini,' I told her.

"She said, 'You're tall for an Italian.'

"I said, 'My mom's side's Irish.'

"She turned to Honor and said: 'Honor! Give Warren the Irish-Italian waiter my number.' And she did, and the rest is history. Many years have passed, there have been other women. But she was the great love of my life."

The next morning, I remembered that Aunt Theo's letter had said, "Report back to me your progress." She was expecting me to write her a letter. But, oh dear—on what? I didn't have any stationery. So I found this great Italian stationery store called Il Papiro, up on Lexington Avenue. Clover had told me all about it when I told her I needed to get stationery, and I'd been excited to check it out. Once I finally got there, I chose this cream paper with two lonesome-looking silver swans printed on the bottom. And then a navy-blue pen. I'd never had a fancy pen before, but I thought that when you wrote to Theodora Bell, you couldn't use just any old pen.

But that night Val saw me writing the letter and said, "Oh God, Franny, are you writing a *letter*? I mean, letters are okay for an old lady like Aunt Theo, but for you? Nobody sends letters anymore."

"Just because nobody does a thing anymore," I said, "doesn't mean it isn't worth it to do."

"But the world changes! Why not keep up with it?"

"Clover says—"

"Oh," Val threw up her hands, "Clover says, Clover says, Theo says! I mean, I'm so glad Aunt Theo let us come to New York for the summer and all, but honestly, sometimes I feel like we're living in, I don't know, a *museum* in her apartment."

"But who wouldn't want to live in a museum?" I asked. "Remember how when we were little we wanted to go live in the Palace of Fine Arts?" That's in this absolutely beautiful old building in San Francisco. "Remember, we wanted to go and put a tent up on the grounds, and feed the swans in the lagoon?"

"Yes," said Val, "but, Franny, we were just children then."

I paused. I supposed she had a point.

Here's what I decided to write.

Dear Aunt Theodora,

Reporting on so-called progress. Valentine suggested the Plaza. Can you believe it? When everybody knows it's owned by Donald Trump. Luckily I came up with Bemelmans Bar.

When I go to a place like that, I start to see what you mean about California having no true style to speak of.

Anyway, they sent us dessert and everything was just divine.

Oh, we met your old flame Warren. He says hello.

XXX
Frances

P.S. Please, Aunt Theodora, I think I should let you know I've just about filled the beautiful pink-and-gray journal you sent me from Paris. Would it be too bold to ask for another?

A week passed, and a package for me appeared in the mail. It was the same type of journal, but different colors, darker and richer this time, not pink-and-gray but plum suede with mauve pages. I couldn't help but notice they were more like the colors Aunt Theo would choose for herself. A woman's and not a girl's.

The letter she had enclosed with the package had two words of advice: "Take notes."

8

Ballet Lessons

$\mathcal{T}$hen Valentine fell in love, which of course is what we'd both been waiting for.

It happened this way.

Ever since we went to the Carlyle and Warren flirted with her, she'd been pretty much insufferable, flouncing around the apartment in her underwear and making mysterious faces in the mirror.

"Put some clothes on, Val," I told her.

"Oh, just because you don't have any boobs yet," she said, which I think was absolutely uncalled for.

Incredibly enough, she went on, "Of course you might be one of those women who never really gets boobs. But that's okay. There are so many different kinds of clothes you'll be able to wear."

"Val."

"Well, just ask Clover. She was saying it used to be so hard going shopping with Aunt Theo, because, you know, Aunt Theo's so tall and skinny and used to be a model and all and Clover's so short. But Aunt Theo always made her feel better by saying that she, Clover I mean, had the kind of body that looks prettiest naked."

"*Val!*"

"Suit yourself," she said, and went back to applying her eyeliner in the mirror. It was Saturday morning, and she was getting ready to go to this ballet class at Lincoln Center. The reason for that was because an old friend of Aunt Theo's turned out to be a former ballerina who now taught classes there for beginners. Clover had arranged for us to attend her classes for free if we wanted, but only Valentine wanted to; I did ballet once when I was little and wasn't any good at it, so I didn't want to make that mistake again. But Valentine loves dancing and was excited to give it a try.

"If you don't finish up with that, you're going to be late," I warned her.

"Oh, hush! There might be boys there."

"In *ballet* class?"

"Just, you know, around," she said mysteriously.

After class, Valentine and I had planned to meet at this tearoom on the Upper East Side called Sant Ambroeus. Clover had recommended it to me earlier that morning, thinking that we would be sure to enjoy it. Valentine was walking across the park to meet me, and so I got there before her and had a chance to take it all in. You know something? I kind of like eating in restaurants alone. There is such opportunity for observation then. When you're with someone else, you don't notice things the same way.

Clover had recommended Sant Ambroeus because it's Italian, Milanese to be exact, and very old. It seems like everywhere Clover recommends is old but has style. Sant Ambroeus definitely does. The pastries are in shining cases and there are crystal chandeliers.

The waiters wear pink shirts and black pants and all seem to be just incredibly handsome. One young man filling water glasses looked a bit like a piece of ancient sculpture.

Oh, when I go to college the first thing I want to do is take Italian! Aunt Theo and Clover speak it from going abroad so much. I don't think it will be too, too hard for me to pick up since I'm fluent in French already. Here were some of the beautiful-sounding words on the menu: *Asparagi Freddi, Polipo al Profumo de Limone, Vitello Tonnato* . . .

"Franny, what are you doing, talking to yourself?"

I looked up and saw Val. Her black leotard was sliding off her shoulders and her twist was coming undone. If she hadn't been so gorgeous, I would have felt embarrassed to be seen with her in the dining room of Sant Ambroeus.

"Oh," I said, caught, "you'll think it silly, but I was just practicing my Italian."

"*Your* Italian, Franny? You make it sound like you already speak it! Well, tell Mom and Dad you want to learn it, and see if they'll fit it into your schedule. Just imagine"—Val sighed all melodramatically—"going back home, and having to do homework, and activities, and Girls Chorus." Then she picked up a menu and said, "God, Franny, you expect me to eat *octopus* when I'm in love?"

"You mean *Polipo al Profumo* . . ." I began, showing off my accent *and* knowing full well that it annoyed her I didn't ask right away about the guy, whoever he was.

"Well, I just can't eat when I'm feeling all light and breathless . . ."

"Oh." I couldn't imagine ever being in such an emotional

condition that I wasn't fond of eating. Especially here, at Sant Ambroeus!

"Aren't you going to ask me?" she demanded.

"All right, Val. Who is he?"

"His name is Julian," she said, with a proud lift of her head. "He has dark hair and blue eyes."

"Oh," I said. I did have to admit that was an attractive, and rare, combination.

Julian. I pondered the name. "*Wavy* dark hair," she went on. "And *deep* blue eyes. And he was carrying a cello. Turns out he goes to Juilliard. That's just about impossible to get into!"

"I know, I know."

"You have to be, like, a genius—"

"Where did you meet him?"

"Well—it was right after I got out of ballet class. Oh, I'll tell you about what happened in class later! But anyway. It was after class and I walked outside and went to sit down by that fountain they have, the big one that's all lit up at night. I was just sitting there when I noticed this cute boy with a cello, and I started looking at him, and then he started looking at me too. And then he came over and talked to me!"

"What did he say?"

"'Are you a dancer?' is what he said."

"And what did you say?"

"I said yes."

"Val!"

"Whatever."

"But you know he must just assume you're a ballerina?"

She tossed her head and said, "Well, what of it? If you were a man, wouldn't you fall in love with a ballerina?"

I had to admit she had a point. When it came to Love, ballerinas had the edge over the rest of us.

"Val, how old is he?" I asked.

"Twenty-one."

Twenty-one! The perfect age, it seemed to me, for any cute boy to be. I thought it only appropriate that one's first love should be a couple years older anyway. And definitely not younger: no way.

"How old does he think you are?"

"Well," said Valentine, "I'm not exactly sure, but he thinks I go to the ballet school."

I looked at Valentine sitting across from me, and I understood that she now lived in a different world from me. It was the world of being a beautiful young woman, a world in which dark-haired, blue-eyed strangers carrying cellos saw you and felt compelled to speak to you out of nowhere. And it was also a world, I saw, of small lies. But lies were important when one was in love. The truth, not so much. I saw that now.

Our food arrived: egg salad and tomato sandwiches, and ones with chicken salad and lemon zest. For tea, we got a pot of something called Vanilla Darjeeling Royal.

"You know what, Franny?" said Valentine, reaching for a sandwich and popping it into her mouth in one bite. I always take tiny bites of tea sandwiches, to make them last longer. "Maybe being in love is all right for your appetite after all. This is *delish*."

We ate our food and sipped our Vanilla Darjeeling Royal tea and were perfectly happy. One of those meals to remember, I was thinking. Aunt Theo was quite right to tell me to "take notes." And afterward when we got back to the apartment I did. As I was writing up the afternoon's events in my journal, for the first time ever I thought to myself that maybe someday I would write a novel too.

9

The Fifi or the Framboise?

"So you're in love," said Clover that evening. "Is it the first time?"

Valentine nodded gravely that it was.

"Well," said Clover calmly, as if she were a priestess overseeing an initiation ritual of some kind, "then there is only one thing to be done."

"What?"

We were both dying to know.

"Lingerie shopping, of course."

Lingerie shopping! The words alone were enough to thrill us.

"Oh!" said Valentine. "Oh! Mom never lets me get fancy underwear. And you know what I want? Black lace, with, what are those things called, garters—"

"It might not be time for black lace just yet," said Clover. "We'll have to see. But we'll get you something, and whatever it is, it will be beautiful."

Valentine looked a bit sulky, because I knew she thought that black lace was just the thing, the only thing, when it came to lingerie.

"We'll go shopping tomorrow," said Clover. "We'll make a day of it. But one thing to keep in mind, girls: just because I'm taking you lingerie shopping doesn't mean that I expect you to wear it in front of somebody. Not necessarily and not by any means soon. I'm taking you lingerie shopping because lingerie is something for *you*. Not for a man. If there's a man, that's just a perk, but not the point. Understand?"

But I don't think poor Val did, because later that night, when we were lying in our twin beds, she said, "What was Clover talking about, anyway? I'm *so* going to show Julian my lingerie."

I rather wanted to tell her that I saw Clover's point. But I didn't, because I thought she'd only say that I was fourteen and didn't have any boobs yet or anyone to show them to anyway. And you know what? She would have been right.

The next morning, Clover appeared at the foot of the staircase in a white cotton dress and this wonderful pale blond straw hat with a navy grosgrain ribbon. On her hands were a pair of little white gloves. I thought she looked like a most beautiful chaperone.

"No trousers please," she said.

"But my green skirt's dirty!" exclaimed Valentine, who was wearing a white T-shirt and black leggings, with her hair up in a messy bun. Perhaps she was thinking that if she ran into Julian, she'd better continue to look like a ballet dancer.

"Oh, all right," said Clover. "Be glad Theo's not here yet. When I was younger, she always made me dress up whenever we went shopping. When I was around Franny's age or maybe a little younger, we used to dress up and go to the Armani store. Theo looks marvelous in Armani. She'd leave her credit card at home, and we'd pretend I was a young heiress from Denmark and that

Theo was my British governess. So I'd get to try on all the clothing, see. We never bought anything but we did make them believe we were serious. Then I grew up and I didn't really fit into Armani anymore."

Clover sighed, remembering.

"Why not?" asked Valentine. "Shouldn't you have fit into it *better*, once you grew up?"

"Oh, no," said Clover, "not once I got my shape. Armani is for tall, narrow people. But who cares? There's always lingerie! Come on, you two."

We went outside and stopped for "caffeine, God help me," said Clover. Once she was caffeinated, she said, "Now. I suggest we do a tour. Like you do with museums. The art of undergarments. The demure and the not so demure."

"The *not* so demure, please," said Valentine.

"That settles it then. Demure it is, to begin with."

So the first store we went to was this tiny place in the Village that looked like a country store, with creaky wooden floors and everything smelling like lavender and sage. It mostly sold men's button-down cotton shirts and women's cotton dresses in pale, subtle colors, so we saw right away why Clover liked it.

"Is this where you get your dresses?" I asked her.

"A lot of them. Beautiful cotton is my favorite thing. Feel this." She rubbed the sleeve of a blush-colored peasant dress. "See, you could make the most divine sheets out of that, no?"

I rubbed it, and it was heavenly.

"And see, these are the underpants they make."

She gestured to a wooden barrel filled with white ruffled underpants in the softest cotton imaginable, and on the white backdrop were scattered various patterns: seersucker, bluebells, sun-washed plaids.

But Valentine said, "But cotton is *boring*. Where's the lacy stuff?"

The salesman said, "Sorry, all of our stuff is cotton. It's a hundred percent organic and it's made right here in New York."

Although Valentine left the store still thoroughly unconvinced that cotton could be sexy, she did say as soon as we got outside, "That salesguy was *cute*."

I said I thought so too.

Clover said, "Yes, but I am afraid that he is not of the heterosexual persuasion."

I am afraid that he is not of the heterosexual persuasion. I made a note of this phrase, to take it back to San Francisco. My friends would be so impressed—so much more ladylike than saying, *Too bad, I think that guy's gay.*

Following Clover's lead, we found ourselves in SoHo, "which is where the edgier stuff is," Clover explained. "Oh, good," said Valentine.

First stop, a store on Mercer Street.

"Now this is more like it," said Valentine when we walked inside.

"I thought you would think so," said Clover. "As a matter of fact, their stuff isn't exactly *my* cup of tea. Some of those more traditional places, like up on Lexington, have truly exquisite European things. That's where Theo and I go for our robes. Theo has this blue-and-white crepe de chine one she used to always wear in the summer, in Sag Harbor, when I was a girl. She was always very big on having the proper cover-up. One of her favorite sayings was: 'Little girls should not be seen at breakfast-time without their wrappers.' "

"Do we have to get wrappers then?" I asked.

"No, silly," said Val, before Clover could answer.

"Well . . ." Clover considered this carefully. "It might be nice if you did, actually, for when she comes to visit. She *is* staying in the apartment after all."

"When is she coming again?" Val yawned.

"August," I said. "August 14." I was so looking forward to it—no way could I have forgotten the exact date.

Clover gestured to the lingerie on the racks and said: "For your more flamboyant tastes, Valentine. I thought you'd like to go someplace a little more *new* for a change. And since you're in love, you must be treated with the utmost gentleness."

"Gentleness?" said Val, not getting it. "But I've never felt happier in my whole life! Being in love and all."

"Oh," said Clover, with her light little laugh. "Happiness! But happiness is the most fragile thing in the world."

Before we could ponder that one we got carried away by all the bright, beautiful things in the store. The inside was all pink and black and reminded me of the bedroom an old movie star might have. The salesgirls all wore the same thing: these pink button-down dresses with fishnets and spiky gold heels. The dresses were almost like men's shirts and made me think they weren't wearing anything else. But that was silly, I told myself. It was a lingerie store, so of course they must have been wearing lingerie underneath. There was a dizzying array of it—bras, panties, garters, things I couldn't even name—all over the store.

Valentine immediately gravitated to a strawberry-pink one-piece edged in black lace. It was sort of like a bathing suit except it was satin. On what occasion would one be wearing *that?* I wondered.

"One doesn't begin with teddies," said Clover, shooing Valentine away.

Teddies: so that's what the one-piece satin numbers were called. I made a note of the name. Just another thing to bring back to San Francisco with me.

Valentine said, "But . . ." I could tell she *really* wanted that teddy. She was looking at it as though it were a wonderful, melting bar of milk chocolate.

"I think what you need is a special matching bra and undie set that fits really well and makes you feel like magic when you put it on. And for you, Franny, I was thinking of a pretty little nightie. Would you like that?"

I absolutely loved Clover at that moment. For one thing, she had not forgotten me. For another, she understood that I was not quite ready for serious lingerie, but that I still wanted something. And I hated the thought of spending money on an expensive bra when I was still hoping my boobs would grow.

"But not *here* for your nightie, I don't think," Clover went on. "You want something more—sophisticated. I know just the place."

"This *is* sophisticated," said Valentine.

"No, it's not," said Clover firmly. "It's glamorous. There's a difference."

"But glamorous and sophisticated are the same thing."

"Not at all, Valentine. Not at all."

The lingerie sets all had names: the Cara, the Fifi, the Framboise, the Nikita. Valentine tried them all on, and in the end, it was between the Fifi and the Framboise. The Framboise was champagne-pink satin with a black Chantilly lace overlay, but the Fifi, the Fifi was pleated tulle, not satin, and it had ruffles. The Fifi won.

"But how are you going to wear those underneath your clothing?" I asked, looking at the Fifi underpants, which had pleats and ruffles exploding all around the bottom. They were certainly pretty, the prettiest pair of underpants I had ever seen, but . . .

"Who cares?" said Valentine. "I'm just going to wear them around the room. I'm going to wear them *all the time*."

Oh dear. I suddenly had visions of her striking ballet poses in them in front of the mirror. How insufferable *that* would be!

When we were outside again, with Valentine merrily swinging her shopping bag, she said, "Julian has dark hair and blue eyes. Did I tell you? *Wavy* dark hair and *deep* blue eyes."

"You did," said Clover with extraordinary patience. "But tell me more."

We walked along the streets of SoHo till we got to Clover's next destination, which was on Greene Street. It was very different from the previous store, and I saw right away what Clover meant about it being more sophisticated. It was almost more like a museum than a store, done in a palette of mauves and almonds. There were black-and-white photographs on the wall and display cases with delicate, indeterminate objects. I thought they must have been miniature sculptures, but what were sculptures doing in a lingerie store?

"Cool!" said Valentine. I turned around and saw that she was trying on a black satin cat-eye eye mask. Then she took off the eye mask and said, "Oh my God, Franny, look!"

I looked and saw that she was pointing at a display of white cotton underpants. At first glance, they all appeared to be the same and very innocent-looking, almost like what Valentine and I used to wear when we were little girls, but then on the backs black cursive letters spelled out different words: *Aime-Moi, Touche-Moi, Attache-Moi* . . .

"Oh, I forgot you two speak French," said Clover, with a twinkle. "Come along, girls."

What Clover chose for me eventually was the Amour Baby-Doll in Wild Rose. It had tiers of chiffon and was trimmed in nude lace. I had never owned anything so exquisite in my entire life. The color was just right and reminded me of something Aunt Theo would choose.

For herself, Clover bought a pair of silk stockings, white, not black, with lace on top.

"Why can you get stockings and I can't?" asked Valentine.

"Stockings come later," said Clover.

"Later? Later *when?*"

"Later on in a woman's life."

"Oh my God," squealed Valentine, "I can't wait!"

10

Valentine's Knee

*F*or the next several days, there was no word from Julian, and poor Val looked like she was going to *perish* (Clover's word) of waiting. This was what all the songs I loved meant about being in love being full of pain: just to look at Val's face every night before we got into our twin beds. She looked *sunk*. And then when we turned off the lamp every night, I'd hear her let out this great big sorrowful sigh.

But then, the most wonderful thing! A surprise! A phone call. A real, what Clover called a *proper*, phone call, inviting her on a real, a *proper*, date. Since Julian was a cellist, what he had in mind was a musical evening. He took Val to this place called Barge Music, just over the Brooklyn Bridge, where the orchestra played chamber music floating out there on a barge in the East River. They heard a Russian program, which was very emotional, Val said, telling Clover and me all about it later. Which was why when Julian took her out on the roof-deck during intermission and took her in his arms and *kissed her all of a sudden*, with a view of the whole skyline winking behind them, she just couldn't resist.

I thought that Clover might object to this—Val letting

herself be kissed on the first date. I thought back to how she had said, "Why not try to place something of a value on yourself, Valentine?"—a question that I'd been thinking about ever since then and planned to bring up with my friends back in San Francisco. So I was surprised when Clover exclaimed, "So you let him kiss you! How romantic."

Val just had this silly melting look on her face and couldn't even say anything. Now you know Val is ordinarily very talkative and opinionated, so that just shows you: love does extraordinary things to a woman.

Finally, she found her voice and admitted: "It wasn't my first kiss, actually. But it was so romantic, it felt like it, you know? Like the beginning of something. There was this boy at music camp— well actually, there have been a couple of boys at music camp . . ." She blushed. But then as if she had gone too far, she explained: "All we did was make out."

"Quite all right, Valentine," said Clover smoothly.

But I was thinking I'd never been kissed yet, myself. There'd never been any "boys at music camp" for *me*.

～◇～

And I can't help but notice, the more time Val spends with Julian, the more she isn't quite so interested in spying on that couple on the other roof-deck anymore. Maybe she doesn't need to figure out what they were doing, now that she's doing the same things herself: they don't hold quite the same mystery anymore.

Now whenever Valentine has a date with Julian, Clover lets her upstairs to use her bathroom, *Theo's bathroom*, to get ready. She emerges wearing light makeup—Clover insists on light makeup only—and smelling of lavender, and with this kind of *glow*.

Meanwhile, I still have to use the bathroom downstairs.

One night Clover was brushing Valentine's hair out with a marble-backed Italian hairbrush in front of one of Theo's antique mirrors.

"I once read," she remarked, "that women's hair is at its thickest at the age of fifteen. *Your* hair certainly is plenty thick. Do you think it's true?"

"Oh, no," Valentine said, in real despair. "But I'm seventeen already. Does that mean mine is thinning?"

Clover laughed as she gathered Valentine's red curls up in a twist.

"There," she announced.

When Valentine had gone, I asked Clover, "Why do you think that is?"

"What?"

"Why do you think they say women's hair is the thickest at the age of fifteen?"

"Oh, I don't know," said Clover casually. "I suppose it must have something or other to do with youth."

~ ◇ ~

I finally met Julian, the famous Julian of the deep blue eyes and wavy dark hair, one afternoon when I went with Valentine and him to see a movie at the Walter Reade Theater at Lincoln Center. The movie was *Claire's Knee*, and it was French.

"They're doing this retrospective of some French director," Valentine told me. "Julian knows I speak French, so he suggested it. Wasn't that sweet of him?"

"He won't mind me coming along?"

"Oh, no. It's time you met him anyway. It's getting *serious*.

And I guess it's some famous film. We can tell Dad we went to see it at Lincoln Center. He'll like that."

Valentine was right: Julian *was* cute, though she had neglected to mention he wore glasses, which rather obscured those famous deep blue eyes. Big black-framed glasses that were a little too low on his nose. But actually I thought they were just perfect for a cellist, a serious *artist*, as I thought of him. Julian, I could tell right away, was just that, serious. Which was funny, because Val had never much struck me as being a serious person at all . . .

Julian offered to buy us both something from the concessions stand. When Val and I used to go to movies together, we always shared a large popcorn with gobs of butter, even though Mom and Dad always made a point of telling us that the bright yellow liquid they give you at the movie theater isn't real butter. We didn't care; we loved it. But tonight, I had this feeling Val would prefer to share a large popcorn with Julian, which is exactly what she did, batting her eyelashes and saying to him, "Oh, Julian, you'd better like butter on your popcorn." So I opted out of popcorn and got some Junior Mints, which are my favorite.

We were by far the youngest people in the theater. It seemed that two kinds of people came to movies at Lincoln Center: old people alone or old couples. Not young girls like us.

Finally, the theater darkened and the movie started. *Claire's Knee* was an old film, but at least it was in color. It began with a shot of a beautiful red-and-white motorboat in the canal, with rows of swans parting the water on either side. I thought it was such a delicate image, like something out of a storybook, out of one of the Babar books Mom used to read us at bedtime, and I sat there transfixed. What happens in the movie is this: The man in the boat goes to this summerhouse, which is on Lake Annecy, in the French part of Lake Geneva. There he meets two sisters, though he meets the youngest one, Laura, first. Laura has dark hair and is flat-chested but very intelligent. I wouldn't say she has a pretty face, but it's what you would call an *interesting* face; it comes alive when she's talking. This man, whose name is Jerome, takes her opinions very seriously. They have these incredible, long conversations about Love. Usually they have them sitting in the garden drinking tea, and one time they go on a hike. Laura starts to have a crush on Jerome. You can just tell.

But then her sister Claire shows up. Oh, I forgot to mention—Laura and Claire aren't real sisters, they're half sisters just like Valentine and me. Claire is older than Laura and very beautiful; she's the blonde you see in the movie poster, wearing a straw hat. Most of the movie she spends in a bikini, though there's this one scene when she's climbing a ladder where she has on this dress I loved, robin's-egg blue, with pleats. I was thinking I'd try to find one like that at the vintage store we went to with Clover. I can just imagine Clover saying, in that way of hers: *Trust me. It's very sophisticated.*

Anyway, the scene where she's climbing the ladder is where Jerome falls in love with Claire, which you can kind of see coming right from the minute he meets her, because she's so beautiful and always filmed in this beautiful, gauzy, late afternoon light. What happens is, she's on a ladder picking apples when all of a sudden Jerome notices her knee. The idea is, he falls in love with her knee. Her knee is girlish and delicate. But I guess it's her girlishness that must be attractive to him.

Imagine it! Falling in love with another person based on their *knee*, based on any body part! It reminded me of this time, just a couple of days ago, when we were walking down the street with Clover. It was a very hot night and we'd just gone to get ice cream in the Village and were walking back to the apartment when we passed this really cute guy. Val squealed and said, "Cute!" so loud I think he might have heard her. "Shh!" I said, embarrassed. "What?" said Clover, totally innocent: she hadn't noticed the guy. "You didn't notice him?" demanded Val. "But he was absolutely gorgeous." And then Clover said she didn't much notice men based on their looks: "I happen to require more information." I took note of that phrase, to bring back to San Francisco with me. It sounded so grand. *I happen to require more information.*

You know something? I think that when I grow up, I'm going to require more information too.

But this man in the movie, this Jerome, didn't require any more information than long shiny blond hair and a pair of pretty knees. If you ask me, Laura is a much more likable character than Claire: she has all these interesting thoughts and feelings, while all Claire does is stroll around in a tiny blue bikini. She hardly speaks at all. So what is the point of the movie? Beauty is enough? Love is illogical? Both of these things?

Near the end of the movie, Jerome finally does get to touch Claire's knee. They're left alone at the summerhouse together and he tells her that her boyfriend's been cheating on her, which is true, but still, it's not very nice of him to just break the news to her out of the blue. It's raining outside, really coming down. So, Claire starts crying, and the rain keeps falling, and it's very dramatic. Jerome sits down next to her as though he's going to comfort her but you can see what he's after—her knee! She's wearing a short black sweater dress. And Jerome lets her cry and hands her a handkerchief but then slowly, very slowly, he reaches out and places his hand on her knee. He starts massaging it *for a really long time.*

The camera pulls away, and you see the lake looking all misty. The rain stops.

That's all that happens between them. He doesn't try to get away with anything else.

But just as I started shifting in my seat, figuring the movie would be over soon, I looked over at Valentine, and Julian was stroking *her* knee. Val had this blissful expression on her face, sort of like, you know, when you take your first taste of Nutella and you can't believe how utterly silky and delicious it is? Like that.

I turned my eyes back to the movie screen. I was getting a little embarrassed. I didn't want them to catch me looking. And anyway the movie wasn't over. Jerome describes the experience of touching Claire's knee to his friend Aurora, the lady novelist. He seems very proud of himself.

So here was yet another message about Love. That it doesn't last? That desiring what you want is more interesting than finally getting it?

I couldn't help it, I looked over at Val again. But I didn't look at her knee this time; I looked at her face with the same blissful, drifting expression. And you know what? Suddenly, for the first time this summer, I wasn't jealous of her. I was worried.

Julian took us all the way downtown and dropped us off at Aunt Theo's after the movie. I knew that Val wanted to show off our address for the summer. When we entered the lobby, she made a big point of saying hello to Oscar, the Viennese doorman. "Why, hello, Oscar," and he said right back, "Good evening, Miss

Valentine." I thought she might invite Julian upstairs with us, but she didn't. She kissed him good night in front of the elevator, slipping away just as the doors closed.

Inside the elevator she looked very satisfied, and I said, "Quite the movie star, aren't you?"

"Come off it, Franny. You're just jealous. Now. Isn't he handsome? Did you see he has—"

"Deep blue eyes and wavy black hair?"

"Well, he does, doesn't he?"

We got out on the seventeenth floor and let ourselves into the apartment. But when we let ourselves in, there was Clover, lying on the sofa in a crepe de chine robe, weeping.

11

Lemon Soufflé

"Carlo," she said. "Carlo's dead."

"Oh," we both said, rather disappointed. In a way, I'd been hoping for some big *drama*. I pictured Carlo's green body, in that beautiful shade of rich clay green, wiggly no more. By now Clover had stopped weeping, but there were still faint tears running down her face and her eyes were red. I went to the stove and put on another pot of tea.

"Where did you find him?" asked Valentine.

"*Val!*" I said. I didn't think that was a very sensitive question.

"Oh it's fine, Franny," said Clover, getting up from the sofa and carrying her teacup over to the kitchen. "On the roof-deck. On that green velvet love seat, actually. I went out there to read my book, and I tried nudging Carlo over, he always did hog that love seat, but no luck. His body was just kind of—*stiff*—and I knew." She wiped a tear from her eye with the sleeve of her robe and went on, "It's so silly, crying like this over a *turtle*. But I'd had him for years! And then, Theo gave him to me, you know," she added, as if that explained everything.

"We have a dog in San Francisco," said Valentine, again, I

thought, not with a great deal of sympathy. "His name is Pommes, like *pommes frites*."

"I know," said Clover. "You've told me."

"I want cookies," Val said. "Oh! I know. Mint Milanos. I have to have Mint Milanos. Franny—"

"I will not," I said. "If you want cookies, you can go get your own cookies."

"How did you know I was going to ask that?"

"Because you're always asking me to do things like that. You're always bossing me."

"I am not!"

"Girls!" said Clover. "Girls, you're normally very well behaved, but I don't have the strength for this tonight. Anyway, I'll tell you what we're going to do: we'll make a lemon soufflé."

"Lemon soufflé?" said Val, pouting. "But I want chocolate."

"One of these days, you're going to have to cultivate your palate beyond chocolate, and lemon soufflé is an excellent place to start. And anyway, I think we have all the ingredients in the apartment already."

"What do we need?" I asked; lemon soufflé sounded just lovely to me.

"Oh, let's see. Lemons, eggs, sugar, cream, a bit of salt . . ."

With a little bit of rummaging around, I found all of these things. Then Clover took out a cutting board and started on the lemons, and put Val on egg-breaking duty. Val sighed first, but got to it.

"I used to make this in Sag Harbor," said Clover, in a dreamy tone of voice, grating the lemon skins.

"Sag Harbor?" I said.

"That's where I used to go every August, with Theo. She had a house there."

"Oh."

Then she mixed herself a gin and tonic and we all went and sat down in the living room. By now it was dark out, and Clover turned on Aunt Theo's rickety old table lamps. They shed rosy light on the room and on all the paintings of the nudes, looming over the three of us.

"What was the house like?" I asked Clover.

"A big brown Victorian," said Clover, remembering. "With blue shutters."

"Blue and brown together," sniffed Valentine. "That doesn't sound very pretty."

"Oh, no, it was, Valentine, it was. A kind of a rich, fudge brown with Tiffany blue shutters."

"What shade's Tiffany blue again?" asked Val, still unconvinced.

I rolled my eyes.

"Like the store, Val. The color of the boxes the jewelry comes in."

"Oh, right. *That* shade."

Clover continued: "It was one of those old houses that always smelled of the sea and the marshes. And also it smelled like ashes that were left over from last year's fires in the fireplace. Theo just *loved* having fires. She used to sit by the fireplace with these Polish scarves wound around her hair . . ."

"Why Polish?"

"Because she had all these friends in Krakow and Budapest. She was always going over there and coming back with scarves. I can show you some of them later if you're interested. Some of them are quite gorgeous, really."

"Were they from admirers?" I asked.

"Everybody's always talking about admirers this summer," Valentine groaned. "Admirers, admirers! You're just using that word because you heard the grownups use it, Franny. You're always imitating the grownups."

"Am not," I said, though, in fact, Valentine had a point about that; I just didn't want to admit it in front of her.

"Anyway, what I want to know is—" Val tossed her red curls and paused.

"What, Valentine? What is it that you want to know?"

"No, no, I can't ask it. Never mind."

"Oh, don't say that. You girls should feel free this summer to ask me anything, anything at all."

"Well—" She was still hesitating. "What I want to know is how old were you when—"

"Oh," said Clover, understanding immediately.

She's asking about boys, I thought to myself.

"Seventeen," I heard Clover say. "I was seventeen when I fell in love for the first time. It happened in Sag Harbor too."

"You were my age!" exclaimed Valentine.

"Yes, I suppose I was, come to think of it. It happened on a rainy night, I remember. You could hear the wind howling through the pine trees outside. I have always loved being by the ocean when it rains . . ."

"What happened? Keep going," prodded Val. "I want to hear about the guy."

"Oh, him," said Clover, smiling. "Well, I was trying to set the scene before I got to the man."

The use of the word *man* caught my attention, even though it appeared that she was telling the story for Valentine more than for me.

"Man?" I repeated. "Man, or boy, do you mean? You said you were only seventeen at the time."

"Man, then, if you insist. He was older—much older than me . . ."

"How old?" I asked.

"Not *old-old*, I hope," said Valentine. "Right?"

"Older," said Clover sternly, and I knew from that tone of voice that this was as much as she was ever going to tell us.

"Was it fun, though?" said Val.

"First love, fun? Of course it was!"

"But you weren't his first love, it doesn't sound like," Val pointed out.

"Hardly," admitted Clover, with one of her light little laughs. But then turning more serious she went on, "One thing I've always remembered about that night is: the next morning he wasn't there. I remember I got up and I decided to walk straight to the beach. I had on a yellow eyelet dress; funny, I never seem to wear the color yellow anymore. I stared out into the sea and I thought: So this is the summer. The summer I will always remember. Girls, you will have one summer like that too. The summer that you will remember all your life."

I was still thinking about Clover's story by the time the lemon soufflé was ready. It filled the apartment with the clean scent of citrus. When I tasted it I thought it was absolutely delicious, and said so.

But Val tasted it and said, "Good, but not as good as chocolate."

And Clover, with a far-off look in her eyes, said something else: "Not as good as the *first* lemon soufflé I ever had."

Lying in bed later that night, I couldn't fall sleep. I *always* sleep soundly, so something was up. Val appeared to be sleeping all nicely in the bed next to mine. I got up to get a glass of water from the kitchen. When I turned on the lights, something caught my eye on the counter. It was a blue envelope, the same good thick quality as the stationery Aunt Theo used. The envelope was addressed to "Miss Clover Leslie." But the handwriting wasn't Aunt Theo's—it didn't slant and swoop like hers and it wasn't so mysterious or so feminine. I had the feeling that this handwriting—so straight and bold—belonged to a man. There was no return address, but it was postmarked from Rome. I turned over the envelope and saw that the upper right corner was torn. So Clover must have opened it already, which made me feel not too, too bad about what I was going to do. Slowly, the way you pause before you open a present, I took the letter out of the envelope. It read:

Dear Clover,
Coming to the States, and will be in New York for a couple of days. Are you still at Theo's digs in the Village? I hope so, as I like picturing you there. Perhaps with that turtle of yours—Carlo, was it?

I'll be staying at my club on East 50th.
Breakfast lunch drinks etc. etc. etc.?

Your old admirer,
Digby Mansfield

I tucked the letter into the envelope and put it back on the counter. So *that* explained it! Why there was more to Clover weeping on the sofa than just Carlo dying, and why she had been moved to tell Val and me that story tonight, of all nights.

And maybe it even helped explain why Val and I had suspected that she'd been sad about something or other from the beginning of the summer. She was twenty-eight. She'd been in love. She'd had a *disappointment*. But maybe—just maybe—this visit could make it up to her, and maybe I, Franny, could even help her?

12

This Is Not Central Park

In a few days' time, another note arrived from Aunt Theo across the ocean. This time it was just a postcard—on the front it showed a Degas painting, *Three Ballet Dancers, One with Dark Crimson Waist*, and on the back it said:

Dear Frances <u>not</u> Franny,
    C. tells me V. has an admirer. Remember. You are only in New York a little while longer. What about you?

I wrote back:

Dear Aunt Theo,
    It isn't a question of having an admirer. It's a question of finding an admirer who interests me.

Another postcard came from Theo, another Degas, this time a rose-tinted sketch called *Seated Dancer*:

Isn't it lucky for you that my old bean Leander is
coming to New York? That is all I am going to tell you.
                                                          T.

The day I got this postcard, Val was off somewhere with Julian and Clover and I were drinking coffee on the secret roof-deck. Not that it was quite so secret anymore. I think Clover felt guilty about letting Valentine use her bathroom to primp for dates with Julian, so she let me drink coffee with her there as a treat. I think it was so I wouldn't feel so left out. Clover can be kind of a pushover as a chaperone. She's not so strict as that word would suggest.

I never drank coffee in San Francisco but I don't know *how* I'm going to give it up when we go home! My parents started letting Val drink coffee regularly when she turned sixteen, but she drinks it *loaded* with lumps and lumps of sugar. Clover and I take ours hot, with just a *nip*—Clover's word—of heavy cream. (I do put *just one* lump of sugar, which Clover says I won't need in time.) She always serves the cream in a little buttery yellow pot of Aunt Theo's with a cracked spout, so you have to pour it out very carefully.

Clover says I am a *natural* coffee drinker. She says she is not so partial as a rule to tea drinkers, and neither is Aunt Theo, because coffee drinkers, they swear, are apt to have more *character*.

Somehow I feel very protective of Clover now that I know she has *a secret*.

This afternoon, I showed her Aunt Theo's postcard and said, "Who is Leander? Have you ever met him before, Clover?"

"Oh, yes. Many times."

"Well, when is he coming to New York anyway? And why does Aunt Theo want me to meet him?"

"Oh, that. Well—because he's interesting, I suppose, and a man from whom you can learn the art of conversation."

"The art of conversation?" I repeated.

"Why, don't laugh, Franny. It's of the utmost importance."

"Will he tell me about Aunt Theo? He's an old beau of hers, she says." I gestured to the postcard.

"Oh, *everybody* is an old beau of Aunt Theo's," said Clover. "But yes, Leander will certainly be willing to tell you all about her, if you ask."

"Did you invite him to the party?" I was thinking of the party we were having for Aunt Theo's arrival.

"Of course!" Then she took a sip of her coffee and announced, "Also. I've been thinking, Franny. Don't you want something to remember from your summer in New York? Summer always goes so fast! Why, you'll be back in San Francisco before you know it."

I laughed and said, "Oh, I think I already have lots to remember."

"Oh, I know you do, but I mean, don't you want to make some kind of statement this summer? To look back and say 'That was the summer when . . .'?"

I saw what she meant. Val would always be able to say: "That was the summer I met Julian. The summer I fell in love." But what would *I* be able to say?

"Well it's just an idea I had," Clover went on, "but I was thinking about your hair."

I saw what she meant about that too. I pouted a little. "Oh. I know. It isn't as pretty as Val's."

"It doesn't have to be like Val's," said Clover, "and by the way, no sulking. You're also a very pretty young girl *after your own fashion*. To follow one's own fashion. That's the important thing. Theo would agree with me."

"Theo was a *model*. She modeled *in Paris*."

Clover ignored this and went on, "Anyway, I was just thinking I might take you to get a haircut. Long hair is pretty of course, but a haircut, a really good haircut, can be sophisticated. It can add distinction." She paused and added: "Val, for instance, is a beautiful girl, but she does not necessarily have distinction."

That did it. I would get my hair cut.

"Kenneth's," Clover announced. "Kenneth's is the thing."

"What's that?"

"He did Marilyn's hair, and Jackie's . . . and Theo's mother, whenever she came to New York. It's *the* place."

Kenneth's was located at the Waldorf Astoria Hotel, in a beautiful set of rooms with all these cool-looking black-and-white photographs. The staff there called me "mademoiselle," which I filed away to tell Val. "Mademoiselle wants the Seberg," said Clover, adding: "The Jean Seberg. That is, a pixie cut, very classic."

"That is what we do best here," the hairdresser assured Clover. "The classics."

Snip, snip, went my long ashy brown hair I had never liked very much in the first place. Snip, snip, snip, one thin strand and then another. My eyes were closed, I wanted to open them to see the final results. Then I heard the hairdresser say, "Voilà, mademoiselle, the Seberg," and I opened my eyes and stared at my

reflection in the mirror. Clover was right: I was completely trans-
formed.

"I told you," she said. "And your eyes are so beautiful. They
just pop."

"Can we go pick up some eyeliner? Please, Clover, please." I
was thinking of the dark green eyeliner Val always wore and how
dramatic it looked.

"You're, what, fourteen? Too young. What you have is a natural, gamine beauty. Enjoy it, why don't you?"

Afterward Clover took me shopping, "to launch your new
look." We went straight to Bergdorf Goodman, and when I said,
"Isn't that terribly expensive?" Clover said, "Here's what we're going
to do, Franny. We're going to buy you the key pieces of a wardrobe.
Think of it as curating a collection. You will have these pieces for
years, and no going around San Francisco buying cheap little
things here and there with your friends, okay?"

"Okay," I said. I liked the challenge of Clover's proposition: the
idea of *curating a collection*. Val would never have the discipline to
do something like that and stick to it.

Here is what Clover picked out for me at Bergdorf's: a classic
tan trench coat, like the one Catherine Deneuve wears when it's
raining in *The Umbrellas of Cherbourg*; three French sailor shirts,
one black stripes, one navy, one pale pink; two pairs of ballerina
flats, one black, one gold; one pair of black "cigarette pants" ("But,
Clover, I don't smoke!" "It's just the name, silly"); one navy pleated
skirt; and two dresses. The first dress was a cool black linen
A-line. The second one was cream-colored in a material Clover
called "sharkskin" with a Peter Pan collar and big white buttons

up the back. The black dress was very comfortable, but the cream one, not so much. It was very straight and slim.

"It's a sheath dress," said Clover, "and you are lucky to be able to pull it off."

I said the word *sheath* over and over again in my head. *Sheath*. It was so silky and lovely, that word. There was something private about it, a secret, almost. My first sheath dress . . .

We were all set, but then Clover said, "Oh! One more thing. For your hair."

I said I thought my hair was all set.

"But surely sometimes you'll want a bow."

"A bow?"

"Black velvet, I think."

"Black velvet? For summer? Are you sure?"

"*Absolument.* It's very French."

And so we located a black velvet hair ribbon, nestling it in tissue paper in one of my many palest purple Bergdorf Goodman bags. Wait till Val saw me! Oh, she would just *perish* of jealousy!

Then before we left Clover said, "You know, Franny, I think I need to buy a little something too. Would you mind helping me pick something out?"

"Of course not," I said, thinking: She is going to go meet him after all! This man—this Digby—whoever he was . . .

Wasn't it exciting—Clover and I both having meetings with men who were coming to town? She had Digby, and I was getting curious about meeting this old beau of Theo's, this Leander. I would wear my new sheath dress: yes, that was the one.

"Perfume, I think," I heard Clover murmur.

"Perfume?"

"Yes, Franny, I thought I might mix up my scent. It's a good thing to do . . . every once in a while," she added without her usual confidence, and I knew that she was thinking about something. And then she sighed and said, "Oh, no, never mind. I'll save it for later."

"Why, though? We're here."

"Because," explained Clover, "sometimes it's nice to have something to look forward to, you know."

All of a sudden, I saw what Val meant about twenty-eight being, in a way, *old*. Because for Val and me there seemed to be so much to look forward to. I couldn't imagine getting to the age where having something to look forward to could be considered a treat.

Then Clover suggested we take a walk through Central Park and head up toward the Whitney. It was a hot, sticky day, but being in the shade of the trees was nice.

"What's your favorite place in Central Park?" asked Clover.

"The zoo," I said right away. Val and I had gone with Mom and Dad when we were little, and it was one of the first things we checked out again when we got here this summer. "A day like today, I'd like to go see the polar bears. They always look so sleepy and *cool*."

"Oh, I don't much like *large* animals," said Clover, and I couldn't help but think of Carlo the turtle. "I like birds, especially when they have beautiful blue feathers. There is this one kind of bird from India . . ."

But then Clover lost her train of thought when we walked past a little girl having a tantrum in front of the boathouse.

"I want to go to Central Park," she wailed. "Mommy, Mommy, I want to go to Central Park."

The child was speaking in a British accent and was all dolled up in a fluffy white party dress and black patent leather Mary Janes. I guessed her to be about five years old. Her mother was tall and wore her blond hair back in this low bun, and she was pushing her younger daughter in a big fancy stroller, like the Rolls Royce of baby vehicles. It looked to me like a scene out of *Mary Poppins*.

The mother said, "I told you already, this *is* Central Park."

The child put her hands on her hips and announced: "This *is not* Central Park."

Clover and I burst out laughing, and then so did the mother. We walked on, and Clover remarked: "That poor little girl, what a life of disappointment is in store for her! What do you think she imagined Central Park to be like? is the interesting question. Do you think she thought the trees were made out of emeralds or something?"

"The water made out of sapphires," I added.

"One wonders what fabulous visions were dancing in her little blond head."

The piece that Clover wanted to show me at the Whitney was called *Calder's Circus* by the American artist Alexander Calder. Clover says it's better to leave a museum really connecting with one piece than trying to see everything and connecting with nothing.

"This is my *favorite*," she said, sighing.

Calder's Circus is a miniature reproduction of an actual circus. It's made out of all these cool everyday materials—wire, cork, wood, cloth. Because it's about the circus—and because it's kind of like a diorama—what it most made me think of was being a child again. The tininess and the preciousness of it. And you know how going to the circus is such a treat when you're a kid. It's like getting ice cream cake with pink candles. I don't know, maybe I was feeling sentimental that day because of Clover being twenty-eight and having to look forward to a dinky thing like perfume, or the little girl in Central Park who had dreamed, for all we knew, of trees made out of emeralds and what life would hold for *her*. Maybe it was my new haircut, and how it seemed to mark in a very clear *physical* way the ending of one period of my life (little Franny with long mouse-colored hair) and the beginning of another (sophisticated Franny—I hoped?—with her cropped Parisian do). Maybe it was just the characters in the circus. Like, the elephant made me think of a toy I'd had when I was a baby, an elephant named Sebastian, and what had become of him. What had become of all of my old toys, in fact?

Anyway, what I'm trying to say is looking at *Calder's Circus* made me very sad, and I said so to Clover. I asked her if it ever made her feel that way.

"Oh, yes, Franny, my sweet," said Clover, eyes wide. "Every, every time."

13

Belgian Chocolates at the Sherry-Netherland

Theo's old friend Leander came to town a couple of nights later. With Clover's permission, we had agreed to meet at this old hotel, the Sherry-Netherland. Clover dropped me off outside the entrance. I was wearing the cream sharkskin sheath and the black velvet bow in my hair. It was a hot evening, but I loved how cool my neck and shoulders felt with my new haircut. I just felt this kind of keenness.

"Won't you come in with me?" I asked her.

"It's your night, Franny. *Your* entrance."

And then she smiled and waved goodbye, disappearing down Fifth Avenue into the dusk.

I had never been to the Sherry-Netherland. But I remembered it being mentioned in *Eloise* when she talks about there being pigeons on the roof of the Sherry-Netherland, so I knew it had to be near the Plaza. The name had stuck with me all these years because it was just so luscious. The Sherry-Netherland: it sounded like a big box of chocolates.

Speaking of the Plaza, Val and I snuck in there one time just to use the bathroom. (Clover gave us that tip: hotel bathrooms are the best. Just hold your head high and walk in *like a lady*.) Well, the bathrooms at the Plaza must be the most splendid in the whole city, if you ask me, and Val loved the whole place, the deep reds, the leopard pillows, the hot-pink lights, everything. But when I looked around the lobby of the Sherry-Netherland, I knew that it was much more to my taste than the Plaza. I'll tell you the difference: The Plaza is like a big glitzy engagement ring, a new one. The Sherry-Netherland is like a tiny delicate one in an antique setting. Maybe it even has a few tarnishes here and there but it's truly romantic. The Sherry-Netherland is like an old jewel sunk in the city. The decor is soft terra-cotta reds and dusty chocolate marble and dull golds. I *love* it.

Leander was waiting for me at the bar. I knew him instantly because it was August now, the city was starting to empty of people, and there were only a handful of people at the bar. Who else could the distinguished white-haired gentleman be?

I went up to him and introduced myself, using my full name, the way Aunt Theo would have wanted me to: "Hello, I'm Frances Lord."

"Charming," Leander said. "But please tell me that you really go by Franny."

"Sometimes," I said. "But I'm growing out of it a bit now, you know. I'm fourteen."

"Of course you are," said Leander. "But of course you are."

"My sister is seventeen," I went on. "She used to go by Val, but now everyone calls her Valentine. It's much more appropriate."

"Theo told me there were two sisters. She said the older one was supposed to be very beautiful but that from what she could gather the younger one was more interesting. I can tell she was right, Franny . . . May I call you Franny?"

"Certainly."

There was a pause, and we considered the drinks menu. Leander got Scotch and soda, and I got a soda and bitters, which is nonalcoholic but not sweet. I didn't want to order a sweet drink in front of Leander. Val would have done that; she would have had no sense of subtlety. Here we were at the Sherry-Netherland. I couldn't sit there sipping a *Shirley Temple* for Lord's sake.

It was starting to occur to me that for an old man Leander was rather handsome. He had a fine, sharp profile and his white hair had a kind of crispness to it. Actually he reminded me of the Sherry-Netherland itself. He had this old-time elegance, wearing white linen trousers and a brown seersucker blazer, a bit frayed around the cuffs. His butterscotch-colored loafers were old and obviously Italian. Since this summer in New York, I was beginning to be able to identify these things.

"Theo bought me these shoes," he told me. "This one time, in Florence. She was always very generous with her money and I've never had a penny. She was having an affair with a count—"

"A *count*?"

"Why yes. And a handsome young waiter or two." He laughed.

"How did you meet Theo?"

"In Paris. Spring of '63, at a café under the flowering chestnut trees. Do you know the French word for chestnut tree, by the way? It's very beautiful . . ."

"*Le châtaignier*," I answered promptly. Leander looked surprised, so "Val and I go to French school," I explained.

"Of course you do, you creature of Salinger, you! Anyway, I met Theo in Paris in the spring of '63 under the flowering chestnut trees. She had just graduated from Radcliffe and was in Paris working as a runway model. Now that I think of it, her hair was rather like your hair, the same haircut. Very becoming if a girl has good bones."

I was about to tell him I'd gotten the haircut a few days ago and that it was Clover who'd suggested it, but then I decided to let him think I had come up with the idea all on my own. It was better that way.

"Her lips were pale and her eyes were dark. That was the fashion then. But what I remember most about Theo, that afternoon, apart from her considerable beauty, was that she had been crying. There were teardrops on those black Mod lashes of hers. I went up to her and introduced myself. She said, 'It's no good talking to me, whoever you are. I've been weeping.' I said, 'But I am *always* weeping.' She laughed and after that we were fast friends."

"Lovers?" I tried to make the word sound casual.

"Actually, no. Not that I wasn't quite in love with her, at first. Any man would have been. But it was Paris in the spring in that golden era and love was mine for the taking. Oh, the girls crossing the avenues in their plaid skirts, their blue striped dresses! When it rained they wore trench coats . . ."

"What *has* become of the trench coat?" I asked, imitating Leander.

"What indeed? Well anyway. Theo and I were friends and friendship is something altogether different from love. In a way, one finds, it's much rarer . . . more precious."

Now this, this was incredible to me. Friendship *rare*? But

back in San Francisco, Val and I had so many friends. Girlfriends were ordinary everyday entities. Love was the miracle. I tried saying so to Leander. He sighed and asked me: "How old are you again?"

"Fourteen. I'll be fifteen in February."

"Oh, you'll live a lot between now and then, don't worry. By the time February comes, you'll feel as though you've aged *decades*. But permit me: fourteen is still very young. And what an enchanting age it is. You'll find, as time goes on, that innocence is the ultimate aphrodisiac."

"What does that mean?" I had a vague idea that an "aprodisiac" was a fancy word having something to do with sex.

"Aphrodisiac, from the goddess Aphrodite. Presumably your schooling has encompassed the Greek myths? So an aphrodisiac is a substance that is said to heighten desire. Oysters are a rather clichéd example. But for me a better way to look at it is that an aphrodisiac heightens eros, love, beauty. And furthermore, an aphrodisiac must be personal. To each their own. So for me, an aphrodisiac might be a certain flavor bubble bath my Danish wife, Annebirgitte, used to use when we were first married. Annebirgitte, say it to yourself, Franny, it is a very beautiful name. The bubble bath she used was pine. It smelled of the woods when I was first courting her."

"I don't think I have any yet," I said.

"Any what?"

"Aphrodisiacs."

"You do, or shall I say . . . you will soon. I should think that this summer . . ."

"What about this summer?"

"Well, being here, in New York, under Theodora Bell's tender tutelage . . ."

"There was something you said earlier, Leander."

"Yes?"

"You said that when you met Theo that afternoon in Paris in the café, she had been *weeping*. But I just can't see Theo ever *weeping*."

Leander laughed. "Precocious! How precocious this one is. You are quite right, Franny, quite right."

"I think of Theo as being . . . almost inhuman. You know, terribly glamorous and sharp and jaded and all that."

"Oh, yes, oh, yes. I'll tell you what, Franny! Are you hungry? I know I am! Let's order chicken salad sandwiches, why don't we?"

"Chicken salad sandwiches? I didn't see them on the menu." I had seen oysters, shrimp cocktail, and extraordinarily expensive cheeseburgers. What is it about New York City and paying so much for cheeseburgers, anyway?

"We're in one of the finest hotels in one of the finest cities in the world, are we not? Do they not have chicken? Mayonnaise? Bread? Lettuce? Could they not whip up the, if anything, quite modest meal of my fantasies and in doing so transport me to the past?"

And so they did. And Leander was right: a simple cold chicken salad sandwich on toasted white bread can be delicious. After we finished our sandwiches, the bartender sent us a plate of Belgian chocolates in fluted red paper. Apparently that was what the hotel guests got overnight on their pillows. I ate only one of them because I was full, so I put two of them in my pocketbook, to share with Val later that night.

Afterward Leander and I said goodbye to each other on Fifth Avenue.

"Promise me something," he said.

"What?"

"That you'll write to me sometimes when you get back to San Francisco."

"My sister Valentine says nobody writes real letters anymore."

"Ah! But that's your sister Valentine. You, Franny, I have a feeling about you . . ."

"You do?"

"Yes. I have the feeling that you may grow up to become a writer. So writing letters will be excellent practice."

I decided that I liked what he said about me growing up to become a writer. Also, he would write back to me, and I just love getting real letters in the mail. Between Leander and Aunt Theo, I'm going to be quite the *correspondent* when I get back to San Francisco.

～◇～

I was putting on my nightgown, my Amour Baby-Doll in Wild Rose that Clover bought me the day we went lingerie shopping, when she knocked on my door.

"You home, Franny? May I come in?"

"Sure."

Clover opened the door wearing her blue-check artist's smock and a pink chignon in her hair. There were specks of yellow paint on the smock that looked like they hadn't quite dried yet, so I could tell she had been at her studio.

"Oh, how pretty you look! Wasn't I right about how important it is to have a pretty nightie? Now, tell me all about your evening."

I tried to think of something to say other than the question that was on my mind. Eventually I decided to say: "We had chicken salad sandwiches."

"At the Sherry-Netherland? I would have had oysters, myself. Or . . . shrimp cocktail, maybe."

"Oh. Are you fond of oysters?"

"Oh, very! The food of the gods, and so aquatic."

"Do they make you think of Sag Harbor?" All of a sudden, I remembered her story of the summer she was seventeen.

"Well, yes, I suppose they do, now that I think of it."

"Would you call them an aphrodisiac?"

"Heavens, Franny, what a strange question! Though to be perfectly candid: come to think of it, yes."

"Leander says there is no aphrodisiac like innocence."

"Does he? Well, that sounds like Leander, all right. Anyway, I hope you had fun? And isn't the Sherry-Netherland lovely? The Plaza is so *obvious*."

I couldn't help pointing out: "Val loves the Plaza."

But Clover only said, "Why not? People do," and kissed me good night before going on her way.

I lay in bed in my Amour nightie, but somehow, I couldn't fall asleep. It was as if I had drunk champagne, when it was only soda and bitters. I was all abuzz. And it's hard to sleep when you are feeling that way in New York, because outside, you know that so much is going on. As they say, it's the city that never sleeps . . .

When I woke up the next morning, I discovered that the Belgian chocolates I'd saved for Val were melted in their pretty red paper cups. It was a shame, but when I told her they were all melted, she said, "Oh, thanks, Franny, but don't feel *too* bad about it, you know. It's funny, I'm just not craving anything sweet right now."

And then a memory came to me of the time we were at Bemelmans Bar and got Shirley Temples and Clover remarked that once she grew up she didn't much care for sugar anymore: "It's just that after a certain point, one finds one's cravings change. There start to be—other things . . ."

Carnival of the Animals

*J*ust when I'd given up on Val including me in anything ever again, she surprised me. Julian had an extra ticket to this fancy event where his string quartet was playing, and he and Val asked me if I wanted to come along. At first, I didn't want to act *too* excited because that would have been kind of embarrassing, but then Clover said, "Oh, that will be so much fun for you, Franny. What are they playing?"

"Oh." Val shrugged, not all that interested. "You know, that piece—the one with the sounds of all the animals—*Circus of the Animals*."

"Oh!" exclaimed Clover. "Carnival *of the Animals*, you mean. Delicious!"

Julian's string quartet was playing at an event at the American Academy of Arts and Letters. Clover says that's a very prestigious organization that goes way, way back, and in order to be a member you have to be a famous author or musician or painter. It's in this big old mansion all the way up in Harlem, right on the edge of Riverside Drive, on a street that goes down to the water. When we got there, the light falling over the river was very beautiful, and

I remarked to Val, "You know how sometimes you can *forget* that Manhattan is actually an island?"

"I never really thought about it," said Val.

"Well, I just did," I explained, "because being here I really remembered. It's like getting—I don't know—a whiff of the ocean."

"The ocean? Really, Franny?"

"It's just . . . in the air," I said. Sounding rather knowing and mysterious, I hoped.

We were dressed just the opposite of each other tonight. I had on my black linen dress and the black velvet bow in my hair. But Val meanwhile was dressed very simply—at Clover's suggestion—in a long white cotton dress. And around her red curls she wore the soft, floaty green chiffon scarf she got at that vintage store in the Village. I thought the two of us must have looked just elegant walking up the broad steps of the Academy. Val's dress looked practically Grecian, the length and the sweep of it.

Also, we were *decades* younger than everyone else who was there. These people were *old*. A lot of the men wore bow ties and the women did their hair in these big upsweeps with Victorian-looking tortoiseshell combs.

Inside the building, there was this grand staircase and these cozy libraries and galleries full of famous paintings.

"See," Val whispered to me. "Pretty ritzy. Julian was telling me that, like, Jackie O used to come to this event back when she was alive."

Our names were on the guest list. We got to wear name tags saying "Franny Lord" and "Valentine Lord" written out in this lovely black cursive. I vowed right away to save mine afterward—it would be a memento from the summer.

Julian's string quartet played in a cool white room on the top floor. We watched them set up while the room filled with people. There he was—Julian, and wearing a tuxedo too! I had to give Val credit: he *was* handsome, the dark, the distinguished, living-in-New-York-City classical musician. The girls in the quartet wore black cocktail dresses.

Once everyone was seated, the president of the Academy got up and introduced the quartet. Apparently he was a famous poet, though naturally we'd never heard of him. He was this funny-looking little man, *but interesting*, with a purple ascot and his arm in a sling. The ascot and the sling just seemed to go together somehow, like they were parts of a costume. I mean, it was hard to imagine the poet *not* wearing the sling, even once his arm got healed.

After rambling on for a while about the Academy and its members and which ones had died this past year and blah blah blah, he said a few words about Julian's quartet and the piece they were going to play.

"We're going to hear the Swan movement from the *Carnival of the Animals* by Saint-Saëns," the poet said, caressing the word *swan*. A sigh swept through the audience. "I know, I know," he said. "It will take you back to your childhood, it will make you melt."

I couldn't help but notice that when he was playing, Julian stared right at Valentine, right *into her eyes*. Nobody had ever looked into my eyes like that, but then, I reminded myself, I was only fourteen: surely somebody would someday. But then, the more they played, and as the music swelled, my thoughts got carried away. You know how music can bring up the strangest emotions? Well, suddenly I had *this flash*. And the flash said: I will never be young again.

After the quartet was finished playing, everyone went downstairs and sat down to dinner in the library. There was endive salad with blue cheese and Bartlett pears, followed by beef Wellington, which is beef and buttery mushrooms in a pastry shell, so pretty much the height of luxury. I found myself seated between the wife of the president of Juilliard, who didn't speak to me much, and a cranky old nature essayist and biographer who did. He was nearly blind and needed my help identifying the food on his plate. Val wouldn't have helped him, or she would have acted a little put out if she did. Val's not so big on old people, but I like them, and I liked the nature essayist, in spite of his being a little on the cranky side. He was wearing a suit, like all the other men here, but the difference was he had on a hunting cap with a very striking green feather in it. It wasn't a playful, delicate feather, like you might see on a lady's hat. It was a very masculine feather. I asked him to tell me about it.

"Oh, this," he said. "From the Texas Green Kingfisher. A fan sent it to me once. That was back in—let's see—1967, I think it was."

1967! My goodness he was old.

Meanwhile, Julian and Valentine weren't even *attempting* to make conversation. They were just staring at each other across the candlelit table, pretty much drowning in each other's eyes.

The dessert arrived, bitter chocolate pot de crème with raspberries.

"What is that?" asked the essayist, poking.

"Chocolate," I said.

"Oh, chocolate. Good! Berries," he said, in a wondering tone, poking again. "Blackberries?"

"Raspberries."

"Oh." He seemed disappointed.

When we got up from the table, the essayist gave me his mailing address, in Vermont. Another correspondent for me!

We walked downstairs and I watched all the fancy old people get into limousines. There were so many of them, stretched all the way down the block! I'd never seen limos before, not in real life. I guess I was so busy paying attention to the limos, I somehow lost sight of Valentine. I looked around and couldn't find her until I saw the whisper of a long white dress: she was the only woman in the whole crowd who had on a dress that color. I guess women must stop wearing white dresses after a certain age, like after they get married. She and Julian were strolling down the hill toward Riverside Drive. The sky was pitch-black now, and you could see the lights throwing these sparkly streamers on it. Julian was carrying his black cello case, and I thought that between that and Val in her white dress, they made a gorgeous picture.

I started to follow them, and finally I shouted, "Hey, Val! Valentine!"

But it was Julian, not Val, who turned and looked at me. They stopped walking.

"Hey, Franny," he said. "You have a good time tonight?"

"Oh—yes!" I said. "But—"

The limos were driving off, and I started to wonder how we were going to get home. Probably by subway. As long as Julian was with us, I figured it would be okay.

"*But?*" asked Val, sounding very impatient.

Mom and Dad had said that whenever we were out late, we should call Clover to let her know when we'd be home. If it was ever *really* late, Clover would come and get us. I mentioned this to Val.

"Well—shouldn't we call Clover to let her know that we're out of the event?"

Then I saw Val glance at Julian, rather helplessly.

"I think—" began Julian, but Val interrupted him, saying, "Sorry, can you excuse us for a sec?"

So then Julian stood back from us with his cello, trying to pretend he wasn't listening to us.

"Franny," said Val, her eyes flashing in the moonlight, "I'm *not* coming home tonight and there's *no* way you can make me and you're *not* going to call Clover."

"But, Val . . ."

"Oh, please, Franny, for once would you not 'But, Val' me? Come on, you'll get home fine and you'll just tell Clover, *but only if she asks*, that I'm coming home later. I'm coming home later, and I'll be *fine*."

I thought that Val was taking advantage of Clover being such a nice chaperone, and I said so.

"Clover's all right, Franny, but Clover couldn't possibly understand."

"Understand what, Val?"

Valentine tossed her red curls and said, "Being in love," as though I were an absolute idiot.

Meanwhile, Julian was pacing in the background and had started to look a little impatient, and suddenly I started to feel very young, and I was very embarrassed to be treated this way.

I turned to see if there were any limousines left. There weren't, but I did see a couple of regular yellow taxis. And then just as Julian called to us, "Hey, Franny, why don't we take a cab downtown with you?" I drew myself up straight and addressed him but *not* Valentine. I knew she wouldn't like that. Trying to keep my voice cool, I said: "Thank you, Julian, but I think I'd prefer to take a taxi back by myself if you don't mind."

"Let me walk you," he said, but I wouldn't let him. I walked off and got into a taxi. I couldn't help but hope that Val was looking at me as I did it and thinking how grownup I looked. *She* didn't have a proper little black dress yet, I remembered, and *I* did.

But once I got inside the taxi I didn't feel quite as tough as before, little black dress or no little black dress. For one thing, the ride seemed to go on forever and ever. We were really very far away from Aunt Theo's, since it was all the way downtown. Sometimes you forget how big New York City is, and then you see it at night from the inside of a car: it's glamorous, all right, but also kind of *threatening*. I got the sense that it was true: I was only one person out of millions in this city. And all of a sudden I started to feel lonely. Not just lonely—sad. I was sad because of Valentine. It was all over, our life together in San Francisco, as girls. When we got back home, everything would be different. Would we ever sing out loud again?

> *If it takes forever I will wait for you*
> *For a thousand summers I will wait for you . . .*

15

Where's Valentine?

"Cash," the driver said.

After all that, I finally had arrived in front of Aunt Theo's building and I had just taken out Mom and Dad's credit card, which they said to use only on special occasions or in emergencies. I figured that if this didn't count as an emergency, what did?

"I thought you could pay with a card," I said. I was certain that you could pay with a card. It was true that until tonight I'd never taken a taxi by myself, but I'd seen Clover pay for them with cards before and also I had checked to make sure that there was a credit card machine inside the car tonight before it started moving.

"Cash," the driver repeated.

"But I thought—"

I don't like to argue with grownups, or with anybody, really. But I didn't have enough cash on me to pay for the ride. FYI, the cost of taking a taxi from West Harlem to the Village? Outrageous! I can't even bear to tell you exactly how much it was.

"Cash, miss. The machine—it's not working. Broken," he enunciated.

I wasn't sure, quite frankly, if he was telling the truth about the credit card machine not working, but even if he wasn't, what could I do about it? It was his taxi and I was just the passenger.

"But I don't have cash!" I exclaimed, and was embarrassed that my voice when I said this sounded on the brink of tears. All of a sudden I felt very young and very alone and very unprotected, and I think he knew it too. I wished that I hadn't let on, but I couldn't help it.

"You girls today, you never carry cash," the driver was grumbling, and then I thought of something. It was so late, Clover must be at home. I could ask Oscar to buzz the apartment and she could come down and get me.

"I'll get somebody to pay it," I said.

"Who?" he said, sounding suspicious. Of me—and I'm only a fourteen-year-old girl!

"My chaperone," I said importantly, and got out of the cab.

"Your *what*?" I heard him asking after me.

Thank God Oscar was there at the front desk, looking as suave as ever, though when he saw me coming in at this hour he did say, "Good evening, Miss Franny, and what are you doing out all by yourself at this hour?"

"Oscar, please buzz Clover. There's a cab outside"—I pointed—"and the driver's waiting for me to pay the fare and I don't have enough cash on me and—"

"Now, now," said Oscar smoothly, and buzzed Clover. It took a few buzzes to wake her up, but eventually she came downstairs, carrying cash, as instructed. She had on her crepe de chine robe and her cheeks were pink.

"Franny, dear!" Clover cradled me close to her; she smelled good, of lavender soap from her bath, I thought. "Where's Valentine?"

"Oh, she's—" I hesitated.

"*Franny,*" said Clover, suddenly chaperone-like.

I gave up protecting her.

"She's with Julian."

"Never mind that now," said Clover, and went outside to pay the cab fare. After the wild evening I'd had, I felt safe and rested inside the lobby with Oscar. When we got upstairs, Clover boiled me a cup of hot milk—something Aunt Theo used to make her when she was a child, she said—and put me to bed, smoothing my hair and saying: "Don't worry, Franny. It's been a long evening for you. Just go to sleep and I'll wait up for Valentine." Sometimes you don't want to be all glamorous, I realized. Sometimes you just want to be safe.

～◇～

True to her word, Val stayed out all night. But then right around dawn she finally came home, waking me up. I rubbed the sleep from my eyes. Beautiful, creamy pale yellow August light was pouring through our curtains.

"*Franny.*"

"Clover is up. She's been waiting for you to come home."

"Oh, Clover! Clover, Clover, Clover. She's on another floor, dummy."

It was then that I noticed that Val was still fully dressed. I looked over at the alarm clock on my bedside table. It was nearly five in the morning. My sister's long white dress was soiled with grass stains. But the grass stains were a soft green and almost beautiful, as if the dress had been gently touched with tie-dye.

I studied Valentine, standing there in the pale yellow light. I thought of a painting, of all the paintings at Aunt Theo's, all the nudes, and how the painters always painted them against a single color, just like Val against the yellow. There was something differ- ent about her this morning . . .

Yes, something was different. Earlier this summer, ever since we got to New York, Valentine had looked triumphant, with her wild red curls and green eyeliner and the way she was always strik- ing poses in front of the mirror. But for some reason, this morning she looked more serious than she had before. Some goofy life force that used to make her my older sister, my Val, some spring in her step was missing. Now I could tell she would always and forever be Valentine.

Without speaking a word, she went and sat in front of the antique looking glass and picked up one of Aunt Theo's good stiff-bristled English hairbrushes. She started brushing out her hair with slow, luxurious strokes. There was a queer, far-off look in her eyes.

I realized I'd been staring at her for too long, and I tried to go back to sleep. Not that I was tired at all! As a matter of fact, I'd never felt quite so awake in my whole life. My whole body was tingling, was alive. It was funny, but it was almost as though what had happened to my sister had happened to *me*. I wanted to ask her all about it; I wanted her to tell me what it might be like a couple of years later when I . . .

I wanted to tell her that it was going to be all right. I wanted her to tell me that *she* was still all right.

"Where did you get those grass stains?" I asked, pointing at her dress.

But she just sat there brushing her magnificent crown of long red hair and refused to answer me.

"Wait a minute. You didn't sleep *outdoors*, did you?"

That sounded dangerous. Obviously annoyed with me, Valentine put down the hairbrush.

"Oh my God, Franny, no. We slept at his place. But first we just kissed outside—a little." For the first time that morning, she blushed.

"Just wait till Clover finds out," I said, sitting up.

"Oh, Franny, Franny, you went ahead and told her, didn't you?"

"I couldn't help it, Val, because—" It all spilled out, the story of the taxi ride, my having to wake up Clover to pay the fare, everything. Well, okay, not everything; I left out the part about the hot milk, because I decided at the last minute that that made me sound like a baby.

"But I thought they took cards! I asked Julian as you were getting in the cab, and he said, yes definitely, they have to. Oh, Franny, I would never have let you get in that cab if I'd thought you wouldn't be able to pay for it. Honest," swore Valentine.

16

Meet Me Under the Clock

$\mathcal{I}$ went back to bed not believing her, or pretending not to, because some fights are like that: you're just not quite ready to forgive.

But then the next day we made up. Everything is always better in the morning, and I found that I couldn't stay mad at her for long. She was my older sister—my Valentine—and I still loved her.

Meanwhile, it had been a while since I'd heard from Aunt Theo, so I wrote her a letter, thanking her for my new clothes from Bergdorf's and telling her a bit about my meeting with Leander. I thought it was a terrific letter and full of interesting details, but she never replied.

The days were getting shorter, and even during the daytime the sun was a little more gentle, and my dresses had started to wilt at this point in the summer; the cream-colored sharkskin didn't hang quite so crisply anymore. When I got back to San Francisco, I'd have Mom take it to the drycleaner. And then the fogs would roll in, and I'd put that dress away, not to be worn until next year.

During the last couple of weeks in New York, I had become a regular at beautiful, bright green Caffe Reggio on MacDougal

Street, dining on the sidewalk alone, which made me feel very sophisticated. (Even though the café wasn't actually that far away from Aunt Theo's apartment! Still, I liked to pretend that it was and that nobody could find me.) I had moved on from cappuccino to espresso, which tasted thrilling and almost *sinister*. I picked up a pair of sunglasses at that vintage store in the Village Clover took us to when we first got to New York. They were white with black cat-eye tips, and I loved the way they made me feel when I sat at Caffe Reggio alone. Between the sunglasses and my new haircut and the espresso, I felt like I could do anything, and nothing would ever stop me.

I also noticed that boys were starting to look at me. It wasn't *every man* like the way it was with Valentine, but still, there were beginning to be some. No one ever looked at me when we first got to New York, when my hair was mousy and long. I guess I must be growing. I guess I must look older now.

One afternoon when I was at the apartment getting ready to leave, I smelled all these delicious scents drifting down the staircase from the private bath upstairs. And you know something? Suddenly I got a little annoyed, because I figured Val must be up there primping for a date with Julian, and it all came back to me—I mean the way she abandoned me that night after the dinner, standing there on Riverside Drive, her violet eyes going all velvety dark purple in the moonlight. (I forgave her, as you know. But some things you just can't help but remember.)

Not that I could place the exact scent that was perfuming the whole apartment today. But I just knew it was something soft, and incredibly feminine . . .

"Oh, hi, Franny! I didn't know you were home."

I looked up and saw that it was Clover, walking down the stairs. And I knew at once that it couldn't have been Val prepping for a date up there—it was Clover herself.

"Oh, Clover," I exclaimed, "you look absolutely beautiful!"

And she really, really did. You know what had never occurred to me before this summer in New York? That the world isn't divided into the *divinely* beautiful women (Valentine, Mom when she was young and looked like Liz Taylor, Aunt Theo) and the rest of us, after all—that all women can be beautiful, as Clover once said to me, *after their own fashion.*

Today, Clover was standing in a pool of bright sunshine wearing a white cotton dress. Like the dress Val wore to the dinner at the American Academy, it was very simple. But where Val's dress had left her arms and shoulders bare, Clover's dress was actually kind of proper and covered up. It had sleeves that hit just above her little gold charm bracelet, showing the pink-golden skin of her wrist. I thought that was just so *ladylike.* The dress went in at the waist and then out again at the skirt with all of these swishy pleats. It was funny. Even though the dress had sleeves, it looked incredibly cool and summery. The cotton gave the feeling of being almost, but not quite, see-through. Just enough to make you wonder . . .

A couple of things were different about Clover's appearance today. For one thing, she had on high heels, which I'd never seen her wear before, except for that time we all got dressed up to go to the Carlyle. And I just had this feeling that women who don't wear heels regularly don't bother with them unless something *really important* is up. I've never worn heels yet, but I always think they must just *kill* your feet!

The other thing I noticed about Clover was her hair. Clover's hair tends to be—I don't want to be unkind—untidy. The thing is, her hair isn't thick like Val's, it's fine like a baby's, so the pieces fly in all these different directions. It's all right, though; I mean, she's a *sculptress*. But today she wore it in a half twist pulled back from her face, and with the crown all fluffed out on top. It had all this *volume*.

I think she could tell I was staring at her, so she said with a little laugh, "Oh, my hair. What do you think, Franny? It's called the Soufflé."

"Like *lemon* soufflé?" I asked, remembering.

"Apparently that's what they call this style," said Clover, touching her hair. Then: "Oh, no! I'm not supposed to touch it. They told me not to dare touch it or brush it out. To keep the volume, see."

I decided to be kind of sassy and ask her: "What perfume did you end up getting, Clover?"

I thought I was being so *sly*, and I couldn't help but be proud of myself.

"Perfume?"

"Weren't you looking for a new perfume, didn't you say?"

"Oh, what a good memory you have, Franny! Why—yes. Do you like it?" She put her wrist out to me, and I sniffed it. "It's vanilla. Or *vaniglia*, I should say. Isn't that a gorgeous word?" She shrugged. "It's Italian."

"The word or the perfume?"

"Both." She laughed. "It's by Santa Maria Novella. They're this old apothecary from Florence. A favorite of Theo's."

"Did she—Theo—used to wear *vaniglia*?"

"Why, yes, Franny, she did."

And then Clover sighed and fished an enormous pair of emerald green sunglasses out of her purse. She put on the sunglasses and said: "Well, Franny, I must be going, see you later."

As she got into the elevator, I came up with a plan in my head. What if I *followed* her? I couldn't help it, I was so curious about this meeting of hers. Besides, I had nothing else to do today, and maybe I could do what Aunt Theo told me and "take notes."

So. Here's what happened!

Clover got a taxi in front of the building, and I waited until they drove off and got the next one. Then I actually got to say "Follow that cab," which was very exciting, just like in the movies. I wanted the taxi driver to be all impressed with me, but you know something? I don't think he was. He just stepped on the pedal and followed Clover's taxi. I guess New York City taxi drivers are used to seeing just about *everything*.

Inside the cab, I put on my sunglasses, and they made me feel perfectly invisible. Just the thing for spying on someone!

We passed Fourteenth Street. Was Clover going all the way uptown? But then eventually the taxi pulled over and I got out in front of the entrance to Grand Central.

Meanwhile, I watched Clover sail through some very grand-looking doors.

"Here," I said, handing the taxi driver money for the fare and getting out of the car. "Keep the change."

Grand Central! Of course. So this was the famous Grand Central Terminal, which Val and I had seen in so many movies, pretty much whenever a character gets off a train and they want you to know: *Here is New York.* Dad's big on trains and he put Grand Central on the list of architectural monuments we should see while we were here, but somehow we'd never gotten around to it, and this was the first time I'd ever been inside it.

Well, *here is New York* is exactly what you feel when you stand inside Grand Central. It makes you feel like taking a deep breath and standing up straight. It's just *ravishing.* The ceilings are high and this wonderful soft, curved shape and the prettiest blue, kind of like a robin's egg. And there are even stars painted on the ceiling. *Stars.*

I was glad that Clover had on a white dress, because between that and her bouncy golden hair she was easy to spot in a crowd. She went and walked toward this enormous old gold clock they have. There were a bunch of people waiting there, but I swear I could tell *instantly* which one of them was waiting for Clover. It just had to be the tall, distinguished older man—no, *gentleman*—in the blue seersucker suit.

And it was, it was! She walked up to him, looking marvelous, I have to say, in her tippy-tippy heels and green sunglasses. And then guess what? She took the sunglasses off before she kissed him, just lightly, not a *kiss-kiss* but kind of a sad, lingering kiss, like the whisper—the memory?—of a kiss. Now I have to admit I don't know much about kissing, not having ever been kissed yet, myself. But I could tell that there must be so many different kinds of kisses in this world. Like for instance, the minute I saw Clover kiss the man in the blue seersucker suit, I knew that the way Valentine and Julian kissed must have been completely different. It was like it had all of these feelings running underneath it, not on top of it, not happy young people in love emotions, like the way Valentine must kiss Julian . . .

Clover and Digby talked for a bit, standing there underneath the clock. I made out Digby laughing a couple of times. So that told me something, without even having been introduced to him. He was one of those happy, careless, laughing types of men. He had—a phrase popped into my mind, and I liked it—*easy charm.* But was easy charm to be trusted?

Then Clover and Digby turned and walked down a kind of tunnel, where the floor started to slope. It looked like they were going someplace very intimate and mysterious.

I waited so they wouldn't see me, and then I walked down the tunnel too. The tiles on the floor were this elegant chocolate brown and everything felt all cozy and old-fashioned. Then they walked into a restaurant—"The Oyster Bar at Grand Central," the sign said.

I thought that when I grew up, I'd like to have a romantic lunch at the Oyster Bar myself. It seemed just about perfect. There was this cool ceiling with red bricks, and it had those red-and-white-check tablecloths. And I loved the way it was just tucked inside the train station like this.

Inside the restaurant, Digby pulled out Clover's chair for her, so that was nice, though I still didn't quite trust him! They read the menu and ordered drinks. White wine, it looked like, when it came. Well, I guess that made sense, with oysters.

Oh, I wished I knew what they were ordering. I looked at the menu posted on the wall outside the door. Oysters had such interesting names: Blue Point, French Kiss, Sister Point, Wellfleet.

Looking at the menu made me realize that I was actually pretty hungry. Then I saw that the restaurant had a bar, kind of like a lunch counter, where people were eating all by themselves. Some of them looked like they were businessmen, with briefcases. Imagine growing up and working in Manhattan and taking your lunch break at the Oyster Bar, just like it was any old thing.

Clover was sitting with her back to the counter and Digby didn't know who I was. So why not treat myself to lunch at the counter? And if Clover did see me—well, I'd just pretend it was a coincidence. I'd whip off my sunglasses and say, *Fancy meeting you here.*

I'm not bragging, but the man at the counter seemed to be kind of *fascinated* with me. Maybe he's just not used to seeing young girls dine in restaurants alone, but I was getting to be a pro at it this summer. Once you get the hang of something, it's amazing how much fun it can be.

I couldn't get alcohol obviously, so I just got seltzer with lime. I like seltzer because it's so sparkly you can almost pretend it's champagne if you want.

The man behind the counter said: "Some sunglasses you've got on. I take it you're not a tourist?"

I hesitated before saying: "No."

I mean, if Val can lie about being a ballerina, I think I can lie about a little thing like not being a tourist. Anyway, what was it Aunt Theo had said? The idea when you traveled was to find a café and pretend that you lived there?

As if the man was reading my mind, he asked, "Are you a French movie star?"

I thought it was better to ignore this comment. Val, for one, would have made a big deal about it. Instead I asked him: "Even though I'm not a tourist, I still want to know—what do you think is the best thing on the menu? I mean"—I thought of the word Clover often used—"what is the most classic thing on the menu?"

"Easy," he said. "The oyster pan roast."

"Okay, I'd like one of those, please."

"You got it."

I sat back and drank my seltzer and spied on Clover and Digby, who were sitting at a romantic corner table. It was so frustrating, because I couldn't hear what they were saying, but I did notice this: they didn't order the pan roast. They were eating just plain raw oysters. After a time, their table was *heaped* with shells. And I saw them polish off *a whole bottle* of white wine. To think, I didn't know that anyone even drank at lunch anymore! Mom and Dad never do. They have one glass of wine each, at dinner.

Then—blame it on the wine?—Digby folded his hand over Clover's. *Very close*, I noticed. And I imagined the warmth of it flooding over hers.

My oyster pan roast arrived, and oh my God did it smell delicious. It came in this big soup bowl with a piece of toast and on top of the toast there were all of these creamy oysters. I was so happy while I was eating it I almost forgot about spying on Clover and Digby, and that's how it happened. I mean, that's how they saw me, when they were finally leaving the restaurant.

"Franny!" I heard Clover exclaim. "Fancy meeting you here."

Now that was annoying, because *I'd* been planning on using that phrase in case I got caught, so I just said: "Oh, hello . . ."

"Franny," said Clover, "this is an old friend of mine, Digby Mansfield. In town from Rome. Digby, this is Franny Lord. I told you about Franny, remember. She and her sister, Valentine, are here from San Francisco."

"San Francisco," said Digby in a wondering, actually kind of hopeless tone, "San Francisco." And I wondered if he was like Aunt Theo and didn't "do" the West Coast. He didn't look like any man on the West Coast I'd ever seen. "But to see you sitting at the Oyster Bar, anyone would take you for a native."

See, that's what I meant by Digby having easy charm. I couldn't tell if he meant it, but he sure made it sound like he did.

Then, as if something had caught his attention, he asked me in this kind of sharp tone of voice, "Are you the one who was born in Paris?"

Why did everyone mistake me for French today? It must have been a *really* good haircut.

"No," I said, blushing, for Digby's eye contact was very intense. "Oh, no, that was my sister, Valentine. I was born in San Francisco."

"San Francisco again!" exclaimed Digby. "You mustn't be proud of it, you people. To me it's a very dull town."

"I wasn't—"

I don't think that Digby was being mean or anything, but I had noticed that the friends I've met of Aunt Theo's all have one thing in common, and that is that they're very, very opinionated. Oh, well. I guessed this was good training for when I finally met her in person, since obviously she was going to be opinionated too.

"Digby," said Clover firmly, "leave Franny alone. Franny is a dear. Franny is my favorite," she added, leaving no doubt that she preferred me over Valentine. There was an awkward silence among the three of us, and then Clover took care of it, turning to Digby and saying, "Well, I guess I should be walking you out. Franny, you stay here, why don't you?"

Now that I'd been caught, there was just no way I could spy, so I had no idea what was going on when Clover walked him out of the restaurant. It seemed to me like she was gone *forever.*

When she came back, she had her green sunglasses back on. But when she sat down next to me at the counter, she took them off, and there were tears sparkling on her lashes.

"Oh, Franny!" she said, and laughed, a laugh that was wistful and wild all at once. "Oh, Franny, fancy running into *you* here, indeed. You know—I think you just saved me from a grave misfortune." She rolled her eyes, and I couldn't tell if she was being serious or not.

"Really?"

"Oh, yes, I think so actually. Before we ran into you, I'd actually told Digby I would go back to his club with him. Too much wine, and all that!"

"And oysters," I added.

"Quite right, Franny. Too much wine and far too many oysters. A dangerous combination. Such a silly little lunch, when you think about it! You know that before we met I actually told him, 'Meet me under the clock!' Like in the movies. I did kiss him goodbye just now, this really passionate, tragic-feeling kiss. Digby *is* a good kisser. But, me and this ridiculous hairdo! The Soufflé!" She laughed rather wildly, and I got worried about her. I didn't quite see, the way Clover could, how things could apparently be both so funny and so sad. "And then there's—" Clover paused.

"And then there's what?"

"And there's the past. That too. You know. The way it just sits there yawning between people."

I didn't know, and I think Clover could tell, because she said, "Oh, I forget, in some ways you really are still fourteen. That's not a bad thing—it's a very lovely thing. I'll tell you what! You know what I'd like to do right now? Go to Bemelmans and have some of those nice cheesy bar snacks and erase this whole afternoon."

Bemelmans was just about my favorite place I'd been in New York, and I couldn't wait to go back.

"Oh, Clover, can we?" I said.

"Of course I *should* be going to my studio, but let's forget about that. Let's celebrate."

"Celebrate?"

"My solitude, of course. Or put it another way: freedom. What I mean is—" Clover paused. "When you've earned your solitude and figured out how to enjoy it, as I do, it's really quite foolish to undo it for *nothing*. You know, Franny, I'll tell you something I've never told anyone before—not even Theo. He wanted to marry me, once."

"Digby?"

She nodded. "Yes, when I was twenty. It would have meant dropping out of college and moving to Rome. It was just *ridiculous*."

"Is he British?" I asked. I thought I had detected a slight accent.

"Oh, his accent, you mean. Why it's a fake accent, you know! Not that he hasn't lived there for years, but *still*. Theo always used to make fun of it, in fact."

It was then I decided for good that Digby was not worthy of

Clover's attentions and that she was better off without him, free to go wherever she wanted with her orange suitcase.

We took a cab ride to Bemelmans. On the way uptown, I asked her: "What is Digby's connection to Aunt Theo, anyway?"

"Oh, they go way, way back. To her college days, I suppose."

"Was he her boyfriend?"

"No, no, I don't think so, actually. He was just a—what do you call it?—a kindred spirit?"

"Oh."

Lucky for us, once we got to Bemelmans Theo's old beau Warren was there, and Clover and I just talked and talked and ate cheesy bar snacks for the rest of the afternoon. I felt very close to her, as if, through Clover, I had gotten back what I had lost from my sister.

17

At the Foot of the Marine Nymph

*T*he day after Clover and I went to Bemelmans Bar, I stayed out all day exploring and got back to the apartment just as the sun was setting. No lights were on, so I assumed that Clover was at her studio, back in the swing of her "solitude," and that Valentine was off somewhere with Julian. I turned on the lights and kicked off my shoes. Suddenly I heard a sob, like a baby crying. But I didn't know of any babies in the building. Then I realized that the sound was coming from upstairs.

I walked upstairs to Aunt Theo's bedroom. The sobs carried through the French doors from the roof-deck. Slowly I opened the doors. It was dark out by now, and the lights of the city were turning on. And there was Valentine, lying on the green velvet chaise longue and weeping, weeping, the way the young girl wept in the crashing rain at the end of *Claire's Knee.*

"Valentine!" I said, and it was only after I said it that I realized it had been a while now since I had called her Val.

She was still weeping.

I sat down beside her in the dark. I said: "Is it—Julian?"

She nodded.

"What happened?"

"He already had another girlfriend!"

She sobbed some more.

"That's *terrible*," I said.

"She's older than me, she goes to Juilliard too. Her name is Beatrice and she plays the piano. They met at some genius camp in the Berkshires."

"Oh," I said, adding: "That's kind of annoying actually."

"I know! Totally annoying."

"I know you must feel horrible," I said, "but it is the end of the summer and . . ."

"And what, Franny? We were *in love*. We were going to write *letters*, and I was going to come back to go to college here and we were going to live together, like in some little apartment in the Village . . ."

This plan did not sound all that realistic to me, but no way was I going to point that out right now. But what did I know? I'd never been in love. And for that matter, should love be "realistic"? Shouldn't love be all about transcending the "realistic"? Oh, I was full of all these fascinating thoughts and questions tonight . . .

Trying to make my voice sound extra gentle, I asked: "Where was the girlfriend—Beatrice—all this time?"

"Oh, she was on tour in Shanghai. She got back a few days ago."

"Also annoying."

"Oh, Franny, you get it! I hate her. What am I going to do?"

"We'll—we'll ask Clover. She'll know."

"Clover? But Clover is almost thirty and she's not married, re-member."

But I knew Clover's secret: I knew that she could have gotten married, once. It occurred to me, all of a sudden, that maybe I wouldn't get married either. Maybe I'd grow up and live in New York, and sit in old-world Italian cafés wearing dark glasses, and be a writer. Yes: I'd be a writer. But now was not the time to share it with Valentine. All I said was: "So?"

"So. *She* doesn't have some magical formula for how to be happy in love."

The city lights were very splendid from the secret roof-deck, and I suddenly found myself in an expansive mood.

"Is that the point of love?" I asked. "To have a magic formula?"

~ ◇ ~

Valentine survived the night by eating a bagful of Mint Milano cookies she refused to share with me (I didn't really mind), and listening to the *Swan* movement of *Carnival of the Animals* over and over again.

"God!" she said, splitting another Mint Milano in half. "You're going to have to go get me another bag of these, Franny, I swear, they're the only thing that's keeping me alive."

"It's the middle of the night," I said.

"It's New York City," said Valentine. "Something will be open."

I couldn't argue with that.

"Won't you be getting all hopped up on sugar? Don't you want to be able to fall asleep?"

"What are you, dumb, Franny? My heart is broken, my life is over! I wish I could go to bed and fall asleep absolutely *forever*."

I couldn't help but notice how Valentine, when she was happy with Julian, didn't want the Belgian chocolates I brought her from the Sherry-Netherland. But now, without him, Mint Milanos were supposedly "keeping her alive." And so among other things this summer, I discovered that sugar seemed to have something to do with sex in the lives of grownup women. I would have to start paying more attention to my cravings, myself.

The next morning, when Clover heard that Julian had dumped Valentine, her "magic solution" was to take us straight to the Frick. She was "appalled" we hadn't already been and assured us, "You'll leave there and feel better, I know it."

But first, we had to get Valentine out of bed.

"I don't want to go," she said, moaning. "I just want to stay in bed and die. Pull the shades, Franny, will you? The light, the light!"

Clover's solution to that was to serve her a café au lait with more milk than coffee and buttered toast shredded into bits, as if it were for a baby. When Valentine finally and with great effort got out of bed, Clover had already picked what she was going to wear, generously offering her a dress from her own closet. I had never seen a dress quite like it before. Clover called it a "patio gown." It was sleeveless but very long and in a silky knit material of different zigzagging blue and green stripes, like the ocean. Valentine, being bratty, was not convinced that she liked it.

"It's weird," she said. "All those zigzags."

"It's a Missoni," Clover said, adding: "Aunt Theo got it for me from Italy one summer. And if you can't see the inherent chic of a Missoni, Valentine, well, I don't know what this summer in New York has done for your cultural and aesthetic education."

At this, Valentine burst into tears again, reminding Clover: her heart was *broken*. It would be broken *forever*.

"Oh dear," said Clover, obviously feeling bad. "Come on, put on the dress and you'll feel better. You're going to look gorgeous in it. You can keep it, in fact. Bring it back to San Francisco and your mother will die of jealousy, her seventeen-year-old daughter with a real Missoni. I love it, but the fact is I'm not quite tall enough to get away with that length."

Valentine put the dress on and smiled for the first time since yesterday when she looked at her reflection in the mirror. Clover also gave her the pair of emerald-green sunglasses she'd worn on her date with Digby, adding: "Those are on loan, mind you. No tucking them in your suitcase. But do wear them today. It is always a good idea to wear sunglasses after a breakup, one never knows when one may feel like bursting into tears. Oh, also, you might get your nails done later." Valentine's toenails at the moment were dark red, but terribly chipped. "And you might," Clover continued, "consider getting a new color. Freshening these things up a bit is always good for morale."

We took a cab uptown, another concession to Valentine's fragile state: "One can't brave the New York City Transit System on a broken heart," Clover said. The Frick is just up the street from the Sherry-Netherland, and it isn't a big museum like the Met— Valentine and I had been to the Met *twice* this summer, and we couldn't get through it. The Frick is in this mansion where someone once actually lived. I always have loved portrait paintings and the Frick has some of the best. One you have probably already seen because it's very famous is *Comtesse d'Haussonville* by Ingres. It shows a young brown-haired lady in a soft blue gown leaning against a fireplace. There is something about her gaze I just love. She looks like she has a secret.

We went to the Museum of Modern Art too when we first got

to New York, but I don't know, I guess I like eighteenth-century painting best. It's so realistic, you can stare at the painting and come up with a story.

There were also pieces of French sculpture, which Clover, being a sculptress, made much of. But I've never liked sculptures as much as paintings because they don't lend themselves to stories quite the same way. A sculpture just stands there, it doesn't let you in.

Valentine acted a bit bratty at first, swanning about the museum and sinking onto the benches in her Missoni patio gown and emerald-green sunglasses. People turned to look at her, and I had the thought: She will be in love again in no time. It seemed to me that my sister was made for Love with a Capital L, though I also knew that, Valentine being Valentine, she would milk her broken heart for sympathy for as long as she could.

"Girls," said Clover, "girls, come, this is what I wanted you to see especially, the Fragonard Room."

"The what room?" asked Valentine.

"Fragonard. He was a rococo French painter, one of my favorites. Come, up, up, up, Val, this way."

Sighing, Valentine pulled herself up from the bench, and we followed Clover.

Clover was right: the Fragonard Room was absolutely marvelous, like if a pink-and-gold valentine could be a room, it would be the Fragonard Room. It consists of murals, which I love, because, talk about making up stories! Murals are the best when it comes to that. The murals in the Fragonard Room are all on the theme of *The Progress of Love*.

"Which one are you most immediately drawn to?" Clover asked us.

I pointed at one mural, and Valentine at another.

"Interesting," said Clover. "Very interesting."

"What's interesting?" I asked.

"Well, which mural you choose says a great deal about your romantic sensibility, I think. You, Valentine, chose *The Lover Crowned*."

The Lover Crowned showed two lovers in a garden of red roses under a lush blue-green sky.

"I did not," said Valentine, to whom this must have been quite humiliating on the day when she was nursing a broken heart. "I meant to choose *Love Disparue*."

Clover laughed lightly and said: "Well, there is no mural by that name, though perhaps there should be. And anyway, you chose the one you already chose: *The Lover Crowned*. Which in my opinion is an excellent sign for your recovery, Valentine. You are not a true Romantic, but rather a true optimist and sensualist. And you have the good fortune to be beautiful. I see a most happy and active love life in your future."

"Happy?" said Valentine, practically spitting the word. "Happy, you say? And I'm *not* a true Romantic?"

"No, I'm afraid you're not. Your sister is the true Romantic. See, Franny, you chose *Love Letters*. Isn't it delicious, by the way?" Clover gestured to the painting, which also showed two lovers in a garden, but the colors were softer and the painting was much more wistful than *The Lover Crowned*. "That pink parasol, did you ever see such a tender shade of pink? A tender sensibility is what choosing this painting connotes—tender and sentimental. The person who chooses *Love Letters* will treasure and remember things. Not so, the person who chooses *The Lover Crowned*.

They'll forget, they'll tumble into love all over again. But also, to choose *Love Letters* means that you will be forever disappointed. It means that you prefer expectation to consummation, and that, Valentine, is the true Romantic condition."

"That makes no sense at all," said Valentine. "A true Romantic would enjoy the consummation. A true Romantic would choose *The Lover Crowned*."

"Oh, no," said Clover. "A true Romantic knows that the inner life is the thing, the only thing that really matters, in the end. And that's what makes the pursuit of human connection so tragic."

"That's just crazy, Clover," said Valentine, shaking her head. "*Crazy.*"

"What's your favorite mural, Clover?" I asked, feeling that the two of them were never going to reach the end of this conversation unless I interrupted it. Clover sighed.

"When I was younger," she began, "when I was younger . . . I think I liked *Love Letters* too, Franny, like you. I *never* cared for *The Lover Crowned*. I think the red in those roses is, I don't know, violent somehow. I have always had this thing against brassy reds. In any event. Now the Fragonard painting I like best isn't in this room, it's in the Music Room. Let's go look at it."

What Clover liked best were three slender decorative panels of hollyhocks. I always thought of hollyhocks as being that wonderful shade of purple-blue but these ones were white and wintry. They made me sad. But knowing what I knew of Clover's life, and how devoted she was to protecting her solitude, I could see why she was drawn to them.

"Boring," said Valentine, who had not forgotten Clover insulting the color red in *The Lover Crowned*.

"You do have to be older to appreciate these," said Clover. "You have to be older and you have to have lost things."

"I've lost things," said Valentine, hands on hips. "I've suffered. I'm suffering right now."

"Oh, I meant," said Clover with a little laugh, "you have to have lost things again, and again, and again."

Was she thinking of her love affair with Digby, I wondered, or were there other men she was thinking about too? Also—and this question was very important—when I got to be Clover's age, would I be the keeper of so many secrets myself?

After this we went and sat by the fountain in the middle of the courtyard. Clover said that this was one of her favorite places in the whole city, and I could see why. I loved the delicate sculptures of swans and marine nymphs, which reminded me of Clover's own sculptures and her "old-fashioned sensibility." But most of all, I loved the gentle sound of the running water. We cooled ourselves by sitting there before going out again into the hot city. A question occurred to me, sitting there:

"What is Aunt Theo's favorite mural, do you suppose?"

Clover laughed, and said, "Oh, that's easy."

"Well, which one?"

"The second mural, *The Pursuit*. Before you get to *Love Letters*."

"Oh? Why do you think that?"

"Because, silly," Clover said, "Aunt Theo is all about handsome strangers and secret admirers. Intrigue; desire; mischief."

18

Thunder!

Clover wanted to take Valentine and me out to dinner at this old French restaurant in the East Fifties called La Grenouille. But as the afternoon wore on, none of us felt like it. It was so hot out; we were in the middle of a heat wave. Clover said that most people who had the money to get out of the city in August did, but that she kind of liked it at this time of year.

"You *do?*" said Valentine, yawning. Now that things hadn't worked out with Julian, she was ready to get back to San Francisco, and school, and especially her friends.

"Well, for one thing, all the summer places are way too crowded right now. I'm contrarian that way. I like to go to the seashore *after* Labor Day. I like the beach in winter."

"Are we really supposed to go out for a big dinner later on?" Valentine went on, sounding a little ungrateful, I thought. But I had to admit that she had a point: Who wanted to go to a *French* restaurant in the middle of a heat wave and have to eat all of those fatty things in thick creamy sauces? And I *love* French food, just not tonight!

Clover, as if reading my mind, said, "Well, we *could* cancel our reservation, I guess. Come to think of it, La Grenouille is really more of a winter restaurant. I'll take you there sometime, though, sometime when you come back to New York."

"But what are we going to *do*?" wailed Valentine. "What are we going to do if we don't go out to dinner?"

"How about the Oyster Bar? Oysters can be so cooling," added Clover.

"Oh, you and Val go. She's never been there before and I have. And anyway—"

"What is it, Franny?"

"I think I'd like to spend tonight alone."

Somehow it seemed to me that this was the best way to truly experience New York: alone. Clover understood immediately what I was talking about, exclaiming, "Of course, Franny! Do whatever you like. Just promise me you won't get into any trouble! And call me right away if you need anything." Ever since the night I'd taken the cab ride by myself all the way from West Harlem, Clover had been acting more protective in her duties as "chaperone."

"You wouldn't let *me* go out and do whatever I like," Valentine sulked.

"Because *you* would get into trouble and Franny wouldn't. That's the difference."

I love Clover, but to tell you the truth, her saying that hurt my feelings just a little bit. Nobody wants to be told that they're *not even capable* of getting into trouble! Maybe that's why, later on that evening, when Clover and Valentine set off all dressed up for the Oyster Bar, I left the apartment at the same time but didn't tell them where I was going. I had on my white sharkskin dress and sunglasses. Valentine pointed to the sunglasses and said, "But, Franny, it's about to get dark out!"

"Not for a while yet," said Clover soothingly.

But Valentine was right: the days were definitely getting shorter now. It was that time of the year.

I'd decided to go and check out this thing called the High Line, which I'd only ever heard of because Julian took Valentine there on one of their first dates and because it was supposed to be *very romantic*. I could even walk there easily from Aunt Theo's apartment, if I just kept on going west. Was it going to rain? I wondered, looking at the sky. Then I figured oh well, I wouldn't mind if it did. The air was still so hot outside, it just might be a relief.

The High Line is this park that runs above the Lower West Side of the city. Before they got the idea to put up the High Line, it used to be just part of this elevated railroad that nobody used anymore, and now it's *all fancy*. Even Clover, who usually dislikes new things, admitted that she likes what they've done with the High Line.

I could see why: it's so nice to see green things growing in the city! I really appreciate nature more in New York than I do in San Francisco, where there's a lot more of it. The colors in San Francisco are pale—California colors—so when you come across something green, it doesn't stand out. But in New York, the colors are darker, and the green stands out so much when you see it. And not just green! I stopped to take in the garden plots. There were soft flowering quinces, and asters, and small star-shaped purple flowers I didn't know the name of, and all these different exotic kinds of grasses, bluish green and rusty pink, making me think, somehow, of the kinds of colors you see in an aquarium. It was all very magical!

I got so carried away looking at the flowers and the grasses that I almost forgot to check out the view. But that was silly, because of course the whole point of the High Line is that it's *above* ground and that you can look down on the city streets while you're up there. I was staring down into the streets of Chelsea, trying to pick out a couple of tiny figures to stare at and make up stories about, which is something I love to do with strangers, when all of a sudden—thunder!

For a split second, as the first drops started to crash down, I thought of how Clover and Valentine would be so cozy and safe indoors at the Oyster Bar and I almost wished I was with them. But no. I had wanted an evening of adventure. An adventure I would have *on my own.*

There are different kinds of rain, though. This was the kind of rain that actually hurt, it was coming down so hard. And wouldn't you know it, I just had to go and have on a white dress tonight. I looked down at it. It was all spotted and practically see-through! Time to go home. I started running in the direction of the exit, or so I thought, when a stranger approached me, saying, "Here, here, come underneath." Then he gestured to his umbrella.

"Oh no, I couldn't poss —" I began. I thought of how Valentine and I had been raised *not to speak to strangers.* But this young man looked perfectly presentable.

"You're soaked," the stranger said. He sounded gentle and, besides, I was relieved to see that he was young—about Valentine's age, I thought. Maybe seventeen or eighteen, tops. I don't know that he was wildly handsome or anything but there was something sympathetic about his face. He was tall, with sandy blond hair, and was wearing beige corduroys and brown lace-up shoes, even in the summer; I've noticed that this is a very East Coast look for men. And I wondered, vaguely, if he went to a prep school.

Was he blushing? Just a little? Why—maybe he was shy. Boys sometimes were, I'd noticed. The nice ones, anyway.

"I'm Franny," I said, putting out my hand. "Franny Lord."

"Alexander," he said.

"Alexander what?"

I became aware, as I was saying this, that I was tilting my head to the side and there was this kind of lilt in my voice. Oh, no, I thought. I'm turning into Valentine! I'm *flirting*.

"Alexander Austin."

"Hello, Alexander Austin," I said, and laughed. *Just because.* "Do you live around here?"

"Oh, no, just visiting. I'm from Boston actually."

"Boston!" I was thinking of Clover and Aunt Theo.

"You've been there?"

"No actually," I admitted. "I'm not from New York either. I'm from San Francisco. My sister, Valentine, and I have been spending the summer here. But Clover—she's our chaperone—she's from Boston . . ."

"Your chaperone?"

"Oh yes. Aunt Theodora insisted we had to have one while we were here."

"Aunt Theodora?" And now he was the one laughing at me. But not unkindly. Just enough so that I knew that he had a sense of humor, which is *very, very important.* "What does a chaperone do, anyway?"

"I guess it might sound kind of silly, but she's teaching us how to be young ladies. Now we wear dresses all the time. We didn't used to, back in San Francisco. Aunt Theo wants us to learn how to live Life with a capital L."

"Oh, I get it now. This is supposed to be your sentimental education," he said.

"What?"

"Flaubert."

"Oh, right. We haven't read him yet. Valentine and I go to French school," I added.

"Ah! French. Would you believe it? I study Greek and Latin."

"In Boston?"

"Uh-huh. My parents are professors. We always come to New York to see exhibits. We came this weekend to go see this one at the Frick on the Turkish influence in—"

"I was just at the Frick!" I said. "We sat *for hours* by the fountain."

"Didn't you look at any of the artwork?"

"Well, some."

"Didn't you get to look at any of the porcelains and bronzes, at least?"

I paused. Was now the time to tell him that really I preferred paintings? Would I have been so self-conscious if I'd been talking to another girl? Probably not.

"We spent a long time in the Fragonard Room," I said. "That's Clover's favorite."

By now the weather had started to clear. It was still raining but only very lightly, and as if reading my mind, Alexander closed the umbrella. I saw drops of water fall. They were this delicate lilac color.

"Shall we?" he said.

I thought of hesitating but decided against it. With a stranger, you don't have to act shy; you can act like anybody you want to be. That's what I was trying to do right now, when I said simply: "Yes."

And then he led me toward the water—the Hudson. New York City seen from this view was timeless; I thought of movie openings and postcards. There was a big white ship in the distance.

"That's the *Queen Mary 2*," said Alexander, sounding knowledgeable and all of a sudden much older than a teenage boy. "The original *Queen Mary* is retired. She's moored somewhere in Long Beach, with nowhere to go."

"How do you know that?" I asked.

"I know a lot about ships. I even build ship models." And now he was blushing again, but there was this kind of defiance mixed in with the blushing, as if actually he was dying for me to be impressed.

"Oh, how—" I began.

"I always wanted to be a naval architect," he said. "But the thing is, the age of the really beautiful ships is past. They don't build them like that anymore. So now I think I'll probably be a regular architect."

"My mother's an architect!" I exclaimed, and had this pleasant feeling of the two of us having things in common.

"What kind of buildings does she do?"

"Oh, wineries and stuff. We live in San Francisco, so—"

Alexander was looking at me with this deep focus, almost as if he were playing an instrument, and I thought all of a sudden of Julian being a cellist. I thought: This is what Valentine must have felt when she was with him. All of this exciting attention. I forgot where we were in the conversation. I was still thinking about lilac-colored raindrops.

Then suddenly I was conscious that the heat wave had lifted. The city was cooling. The flowers along the High Line were blown open and damp. I could still see that big white ship, swaying in the distance.

Alexander Austin, I thought to myself, stealing a glance at him from underneath my lashes. Why couldn't I see him again, anyway? After all, I had the perfect invitation in mind . . .

"How long are you in town?" I asked him. "Do you want to come to this party I'm having on August 14?"

19

An Omelet and a Bottle of Champagne

$\mathcal{I}$ decided against telling Valentine or even Clover about meeting Alexander on the the High Line. For one thing, I liked having a secret. For another, I figured that they would get to meet him at Aunt Theo's party, and when they did, wouldn't they be surprised!

But I thought that Aunt Theo would like to know. (When you have a crush, you do want to confide in somebody! Otherwise it doesn't feel quite real somehow.) So I went back to that Italian stationery store on Lexington and chose a card with delphiniums on it because I was feeling all romantic and because delphiniums are some of the prettiest flowers. And I wrote her:

Dear Aunt Theodora,

I just thought you'd want to know. It happened: I found an admirer who interests me. You can look forward to meeting him at the party, as I look forward to finally meeting you. He will be my mystery guest.

Safe travels and see you soon —

XXX
Frances

As things turned out, there wasn't as much to do as I had thought there would be to get ready for the party. Back at home, whenever Mom and Dad throw a party, they always get all nervous, cleaning the house and making lots of new recipes to impress their friends. But Clover said that what Aunt Theo liked best was for the feel of a party to be spontaneous.

"What does Aunt Theo serve at her parties?" I asked Clover.

"Deviled eggs."

"Deviled eggs and what else?" Valentine wanted to know.

"Just deviled eggs. Or, if she doesn't make deviled eggs, then maybe she'll make an omelet."

"What do you mean, *an omelet?*" repeated Valentine. "You mean to say that she makes one omelet, for a whole bunch of people?"

Clover nodded.

"But that's *ridiculous.* That's *insane.* I would *starve!*"

Val and I do like to eat. Whenever we're at a party with our parents, we go straight for the cheese platter: it's true.

"An omelet and a bottle of champagne, Theo used to say . . ." said Clover dreamily.

"I know!" I said, remembering that it was still the month of August and probably going to be very hot on the night of the party. "Let's have picnic foods. Like, not deviled eggs, they're too sloppy! Let's have hard-boiled eggs and those yummy pale green olives and cold chicken—chicken is so delicious when it's cold, cold, cold—and tomatoes and salt and . . ."

"Sea salt," said Valentine, opinionated.

"Sure, sea salt. And fruit. Fruit for dessert!"

"Figs," said Clover. "Figs would be just the thing in August."

"I don't like that," said Val. "Not that I have anything against figs, but. It does seem to me that if you want a party to be festive, you have to have cake."

"Wise words, Valentine," admitted Clover. "Franny, dear, I think your sister's quite right. If you want a party to be festive, you have to have cake. Even if Aunt Theo will not be likely to eat it herself."

"We will!" Val and I said together, and laughed. Cake is like cheese and crackers. We simply can't resist it.

Leave it to Clover to know *the* place to go for cake. She knows *the* place to go for everything. And when the day of the party finally came she sent us uptown to a bakery on Madison Avenue called Lady M. It was very fancy and also it was Japanese. There were these Japanese ladies behind the counter. Val and I oohed and aahed, and got to taste different samples. There was this green tea crepe cake, which I thought was just heaven—the most *exquisite* soft pale green: like eating poetry—but Val said, no, we have to get chocolate. I did have to admit she had a point about that. So we ended up choosing this type of cake they called "Checkers," which was black and white and really great-looking. Classic-looking, I thought, just the thing for Aunt Theo. Still, who could resist vanilla and chocolate sponge cake with fresh whipped cream? Not us! Oh, I hoped that Aunt Theo would like it, even though—to tell you the truth—I couldn't really picture her eating pastry. Pastry is for mere human beings, and she still seemed to me from everything I had heard about her to be something apart or above.

20

Palazzo

"*W*ho's coming to this party anyway?" Val wanted to know. We were on the secret roof-deck, secret no more, and the three of us were busy arranging flowers. Anemones in particular—Clover had bought bunches and bunches of them, saying that they were her favorite. Anemones are purple and red and white and look kind of like sea creatures. Not as pretty as roses, say, but *interesting*. Kind of like Aunt Theo herself.

"Why, Valentine," Clover said now, "that's a very rude question."

"It is?" Val sounded genuinely shocked that Clover would say this.

"Well, I am only quoting Aunt Theo," Clover admitted. "Once, when I was young, oh, younger than you, I made the mistake of asking her that. Asking her who was coming to a party, I mean. And she said that was a very rude question, and then I did just what you did, Valentine. I asked her why."

"Oh, yeah, and what was the reason?"

"She said: *Because every party should be a mystery.*"

"Hmm," said Valentine, and went back to arranging anemones.

That was kind of how I felt about Alexander Austin showing up tonight: I wanted him to be a mystery, a "mystery guest," as I had said. I saw what it was that Aunt Theo was talking about.

Clover, as if she were reading my mind, said, "A party should be a place where one can fall in love, for instance, Aunt Theo thought. But unexpectedly. Unexpectedly is best."

Valentine said in an actressy kind of voice, as if she were reading a line out of a play, "Oh, but I shall never love again."

Once we were done with decorating it, the secret roof-deck looked very pretty, with its terra-cotta pots and little lemon trees. The days were getting shorter now and the light falling on the roof-deck was already a soft pinky-lilac color. Guests were coming at 7:00.

"And when does Aunt Theo get here again?" I asked Clover, wanting to be ready the second she made an entrance. I didn't want to miss a thing.

"Her plane gets in at eight, so by the time she gets here, the party will be in full swing. She'll like that! She's always so interested, at parties, in seeing who is hitting it off with whom, and that kind of thing."

"Are you talking about romance?" asked Valentine, because this was the important thing in life, obviously.

"That, and friendship too," said Clover slyly, even though it was romance that Valentine and I were thinking of. We were dressed as if we were expecting it, anyway. Valentine was wearing the long blue-and-green-striped Missoni dress Clover had given her, and not wanting me to feel left out, Clover gave me an old dress of hers to wear too—a long pink cotton one that came from India. I felt all floaty and romantic in it, and to make things even more so I decided to wear my black velvet bow in my hair. Clover had on pink too—pink palazzo pants over a black leotard. That was a word I learned for the first time tonight: *palazzo*. I think it's a very striking word.

"But I thought that you said Aunt Theo didn't like for women to wear trousers," sniffed Valentine, because unlike me she missed being able to wear blue jeans and was looking forward to putting them on as soon as we got back to San Francisco.

"But these aren't *trousers-trousers*," said Clover grandly. "These are more like hostess pants."

"Does Aunt Theo have a pair of hostess pants too?" I inquired.

"Oh yes. Hers are black, though."

The mention of the color black reminded me of something.

"Clover?"

"Yes, Franny?" She was now arranging hard-boiled eggs on an old blue china platter. Once the eggs were arranged, she sprinkled chives over them.

"You know how I've always pictured Aunt Theo as looking like . . . ?"

"What?"

I paused to give my words emphasis.

"*Like a cross between an angel and a witch.*"

"You'll get to see her tonight soon enough," said Val, who I knew deep down was not as interested in meeting Aunt Theo in person as I was.

"What witch? What witch are you talking about?"

It was a male voice speaking. Not one I recognized. I looked, and there was this strange man standing behind us on the secret roof-deck. Before any of us could say anything, he and Clover were embracing like old friends.

"Ellery!" I heard Clover exclaiming. "I didn't hear the buzzer. Were you announced?"

"Oh, please. Oscar remembered me from the old days," Ellery said.

"You were talking of Theo, I suppose," said Ellery. "Or, as I like to think of her, Theodora Wentworth Whitin Bell."

"Oh, thank you for reminding me of that, Ellery," said Clover, turning to address Valentine and me. "Remember, Aunt Theo is very big on people using last names. When you meet her tonight, do be sure to introduce yourself with your full names. Also, if you happen to remember, say 'How do you do?' rather than 'Nice to meet you.' Aunt Theo prefers the former."

"But that sounds all pretentious," moaned Val. And even I had to agree with her for once, explaining to Clover: "Val's right. In San Francisco we always say 'Nice to meet you.' That's what Mom and Dad say too."

"Oh, speaking of San Francisco," said Ellery. "Do you know what Theo once said to me about the West Coast?"

"No," we all said.

"She said: 'What would I want to live on the West Coast for? It is too far from Italy.' Italy was always the important thing for her."

"Must have been," said Valentine. "It sounds like she's always going on and on about it. Italian this; Italian that . . ."

"*Valentine*," said Clover, but Ellery merely laughed.

"Aha! I see you must be the rebellious sister. There is always one rebellious sister, isn't there, and one good one? That is, if we are speaking of female archetypes."

"Well," said Val, kind of hesitating because I don't know if she could tell if he was giving her a compliment or not. "I'm the older one, obviously. I'm seventeen."

"Seventeen! An enchanting age. And, in addition to being rebellious, you are also going to be extraordinarily beautiful."

Really, this was getting to be too much. And then I heard Clover saying, "Ellery knows what he's talking about, Valentine. He's been around lots of famous beauties before. He used to be a gossip columnist."

"You did?" Valentine sounded suddenly very interested.

"Oh, back in the day," said Ellery airily. But then I could tell that Val's expression had changed, because she's not so interested, after all, in anything that happened "back in the day," and I bet that any of the names he might have mentioned wouldn't have meant anything to her.

Clover was in the middle of pouring Ellery a glass of champagne when the buzzer rang, and I ran downstairs wondering if it was going to be Alexander. But no—it was Warren. He was carrying a bottle of champagne. "Hey, Franny!" he said, and gave me an affectionate hug. He was so tall, he had to lean way down to reach me.

"The party's upstairs," I said, gesturing to the staircase. "On the roof-deck."

"The secret roof-deck?" He smiled, looking mischievous.

"Wait, do you know it?"

"Uh-huh."

"Oh."

I was disappointed.

I led him up the staircase and into Aunt Theo's bedroom, which was kind of like crawling under the fold of a magic tent. We were sucked into the red walls, the Oriental rug made up of olive greens and golds, not to mention, on the bed, the famous leopard-skin blanket.

"That painting," said Warren, and pointed at the portrait of Aunt Theo over the bed.

"Do you know that too?" I asked.

"Uh-huh," he said again.

"L'heure de la lavande," I said now, feeling like I was a tour guide in a museum.

"Your accent is very good, Franny," said Ellery, who had come over to join us in the bedroom.

"Thank you, Ellery."

He must have known Warren from—what was the phrase he had used?—"back in the day." They were saying hello to each other, and Clover was rushing in to pour more champagne.

"I never knew who painted that," said Warren.

"Yeah, I don't know either," I said. But then, trying to sound all knowledgeable, I added: "I think it was painted in Paris, though."

"Ellery, do you know who painted this portrait of Theo?" Warren asked.

"No, she would never tell even me. And she used to tell me everything, everything!"

The buzzer rang. Alexander! I thought. *I hoped.* And I raced down the staircase again.

21

Getting to Know You

*O*nly it wasn't Alexander. It was—another bottle of champagne? Because here was another older gentleman, bearing a bottle. This one was a beautiful dark green with a fancy pink-and-blue label. *Crème de Cassis*, the bottle said.

"Is that from Paris?" I asked him.

"Dijon," he said.

"Oh."

He laughed.

"Don't worry. *I'm* from Paris, even if the bottle isn't."

"Oh!"

"You are Miss Valentine Lord, perhaps?" He was now staring at me intently.

"Oh, no, she's my sister! I'm Franny—" I caught myself just in time. "I'm Frances Lord. How do you do?" And I put out my hand.

The strange gentleman was laughing at me, but it was a nice laugh. There is such a difference in people's laughs, don't you think? And now I stepped back and stared at *him* intently. He was rather a small man, but still handsome. He had on white jeans and purple velvet loafers. Also, he had red hair. Dark red, kind of like what you call auburn. I liked him.

"Ah, Frances!" he exclaimed, and kissed me lightly on the cheek. "You are the daughter of Milly and Edward, correct?"

"Yes, that's them. Do you know them?"

"From another life . . ." he said, and sighed.

It turned out that the strange gentleman's name was Laurent Victoire, which I thought was just lovely; French names are the prettiest, and I got jealous, all over again, that Valentine had one and I didn't.

"Is Theo here?" Laurent asked me, as I led him upstairs.

"Not yet. She's flying in tonight. Do you know—I've never actually met her!"

"Ah, and your sister—Valentine, is it?—has she ever met her before?"

"No, neither of us have. That's why we're so excited to finally get to see her in person tonight!"

"She is quite something," he said now. We were standing in Aunt Theo's bedroom, at the foot of the bed. Everybody else had moved outside to the roof-deck. "A great beauty. A vision, you might even say! See, Frances," he pointed to the painting over the bed, and whispered, "That portrait. Don't tell any of the others, but I was the one who painted that."

"*You did?*"

He nodded.

"When? Where?"

"One morning in Paris, it was. Wintertime. You see the light

161

in the painting. It's blue. Blue, bordering on lavender. A winter light. You can tell. The year must have been, oh, 1965 or '66 . . ."

Forever and ever ago, I was thinking! A whole other country and a whole other world, and all of a sudden the painting seemed more romantic to me than ever before.

"It's beautiful," I told him. "Really it is. But what did you mean don't tell the others? If I had painted a painting like that, I would be so proud of it, I would definitely want everybody else to know!"

"Ah, but you are not grown up, just yet. You do not know men," said Laurent, smiling. It was a kind smile, but still. I was a little insulted, because no teenage girl likes being told she's not grown up yet, and as for not knowing men, well, I had a boy showing up to see me any minute now! So there!

"Were you in love with Theodora Bell?" I asked him, feeling that it was not every day that I conversed with random red-haired gentlemen who had just flown in from Paris and that now was the time to be bold.

"No," he said simply. "I admired her and her beauty, and I wanted to paint her, to capture it forever. But no, Frances, I was not in love with Theodora Bell; I was in love with somebody else."

Before I could ask "Who?" Clover had spotted Laurent and he was giving her a kiss, and then the buzzer was ringing again, and I ran downstairs to answer it. Clover called after me, "Oh, just tell Oscar to send everyone on up, Franny, dear," just as I was open-ing the door and saw that it was—Alexander Austin! I hoped I didn't blush when I saw him, but I think maybe I did.

"Hey, Franny," he said. He wasn't carrying champagne or any

kind of alcohol, obviously, but instead a bouquet of flowers. They were wild flowers, which are the prettiest flowers to have in the summertime, I think. But really—it wouldn't have mattered what kind of flowers he had brought me, even just plain old carnations, say, because the first time a boy brings you flowers, it's simply very sweet!

"Come upstairs and have some pink lemonade," I said. "I mean, if you like pink lemonade. There's also sparkling water if you'd rather have that."

Alexander said he would have pink lemonade, and smiled. We went upstairs and I introduced him to Clover first, which I thought *only proper*. I was relieved that he had on a jacket, a blue blazer, I guess kind of like what boys on the East Coast must wear at prep school. I knew that Clover would approve of this, and Aunt Theo too, when I introduced him to her later on. I imagined it: introducing Alexander to Aunt Theo. I imagined her being proud that I had finally found an admirer who interested me, as I had promised her in my letter.

"How do you do, Alexander?" I heard Clover saying to him.

Other guests were now arriving. The secret roof-deck was getting full. A gypsy fortune-teller arrived. Her name was Mama Lucia and she had on all red and spoke with a Russian accent. "Says she used to be a countess or something," Ellery whispered to me. "But I don't think so . . ." I was also introduced to somebody named "Cousin Honor," said by Ellery to be a relative of Theo's and a famous modern dancer. She also had on palazzo pants! Only hers were black. I was trying to keep track of all these details so that I could "take notes" on the party in my journal later on. Meanwhile, Warren smashed a champagne flute by accident. He was a big guy and I think just couldn't help smashing into things. Valentine went to get a broom and dustpan to clean it up. I was too distracted with Alexander being there to help her. I wanted to prove that I was a good hostess by paying enough attention to him.

And then Warren started telling this story about Aunt Theo. "Hey, that reminds me. You remember those really colorful old dishes Theo always had, I think they must have been French—?"

"The Quimper?" Clover asked.

"If you say so, kiddo. I remember one time Theo gave me this birthday party here at this very apartment. I was still in my twenties, I was just a kid. Anyway, toward the end of the party, I must have had too much vino because I dropped one of her plates.

"There was this horrible silence. Then you know what Theo did? She burst out laughing, oh, she has such a great laugh, a really sexy laugh, you know, and then she picked up *her* plate and dropped it. It shattered in a million little pieces. Then everyone laughed and we all had more vino. A great birthday, that party."

Now Ellery was competing with him, starting to tell another story about one of Aunt Theo's famous parties just as I was vowing that when I grew up and had parties of my own, I would be a hostess just like Aunt Theo. I would laugh if somebody broke a dish. I would laugh and make it all better. Then just as I was thinking this, Clover tapped me on the shoulder and announced, "It's just been brought to my attention! We're almost out of ice. Would you and Alexander mind running around the corner to the bodega and getting some more?"

She smiled sympathetically, and I knew that she was asking me because she thought it might be fun for me to be alone with Alexander instead of being swarmed by grownups. Grownups are interesting, but only up to a point.

"Let me," wailed Valentine, looking all languid in the moonlight. By now it was officially dark. Looking at her striking this long-armed pose next to one of Aunt Theo's lemon trees, I thought of a dryad or something, some mythological creature that Clover might have shown us that day we all went to the Frick together and sat by the fountain to talk of Love. "Let me, Clover. I'll go."

"Not so fast, young lady. You are going to stay here and mingle."

Val sighed, still managing to look poetic. I had to hand it to her. Then Clover introduced Val to Mama Lucia, which I know Val must have dreaded, because now that she's seventeen, there's just no way around it: she prefers the company of men to that of almost any woman.

"I don't want to miss Aunt Theo," I said to Clover.

"You won't. The bodega is just around the corner. But hurry, Franny. Hurry."

Once we got to the bodega, Alexander offered to pay for the bag of ice. It was a small gesture, but still, I thought it was very gentlemanly of him and I was very impressed by his behavior. It was kind of like his bothering to wear a jacket to the party tonight in that it showed that he paid attention to the little things.

"When do you go back to Boston again?" I asked him. Everything on the city sidewalks at that moment was bright and vivid to me. A cocker spaniel on a red leash; a girl hailing a taxi in a blue polka-dot dress. Even a cone of pistachio ice cream that was melted at my feet. I had to move aside to make sure I didn't step in it, but I didn't mind. Even the messiness of New York—New York in the summer, ice cream spilled on the street, even the garbage cans, by this time at night overflowing—made me think: such richness. That was the same thing I'd felt the very first night we got here, walking around the Village with Clover. I thought it again but even more strongly tonight.

"Soon," was all Alexander said. And then: "When do you go back to San Francisco?"

"Soon," was all I said too.

Because with some people you don't even need words. With some people you can be silent comfortably. You just have *this feeling* about them. It's kind of like what Clover called being a kindred spirit.

Alexander took my hand as we walked inside the building. He's going to kiss me! I thought. And when finally he did, I was so relieved, because let's face it, I did want to get to go back to San Francisco and say to all of my friends: I've been kissed.

But it made me realize again what a difference there can be in kisses. For instance, there was the way that I had seen Clover kiss Digby that day at Grand Central, a sad, lingering kiss. I am sure that there was sadness in that kiss; I felt it. I think that must have been because they were older and meeting again for the first time in years. And then there was the way that Val told me that Julian had kissed her for the first time on the roof-deck of Barge Music, taking her into his arms *all of a sudden*. I think that must have been because they were young and confident. But Alexander and I were even younger than them, of course, and not quite so confident. For one thing, even though he kissed me, he forgot the part about taking me in his arms, like Julian did with Val, or like they do in the movies. Instead he just kind of bent down a little and pressed his lips to mine, and I pressed mine right back. Because, even though there can be such a difference in kisses, your first one is something to remember all your life.

22

Nice to Have Known You

$\mathcal{I}$ was still thinking about Alexander kissing me—trying to re-member it—when we got back to the party and Clover asked Val and me to step away and have a private talk in our bedroom.

"Sit down," she said, closing the door behind her. We sat down on our little *Madeline* beds. Then Clover sat down on my bed too and squeezed my hand.

Valentine was impatient to get back to the party. She gestured to her empty glass. She was thirsty, she said.

"Girls . . ." said Clover, and paused.

"What is it?" whined Valentine. And although I wouldn't have spoken to Clover that way under any circumstances, I was getting impatient too, because I only had thoughts for Alexander.

"I'm going to put this plainly. Something terrible has happened. I just found out over the phone, while you were out getting ice, Franny. Well—this is it. What I have to tell you. Aunt Theo died."

"*Died?*" echoed Valentine, her mouth a perfect O. Then be-fore I knew it, she was crying. It was only now that I noticed there were faint tears on Clover's lashes. She must have tried to wash them away before telling us the news.

"What? When?" I asked.

"In Germany. She was still in Germany apparently. She never did get on the plane. Oh, it sounds like it was very peaceful! She was in her bed at home. She always made sure she had a beautiful bed. She always had all of these velvet pillows . . ." And at the mention of the velvet pillows now Clover was crying too, and had gone over to Valentine's bed to give her a hug.

"Had she been sick a long time?" I wanted to know, still taking it in.

"Yes actually, though she didn't want me to tell you girls or your parents either—she didn't want to let on."

"*Dead*," Valentine repeated, "she's *dead*," just to be as dramatic as possible. Clover reached out and patted her head.

"I guess this won't be so much of a *Getting to Know You* party after all," Clover managed to say between her tears. I wasn't crying yet, and I wondered why that should be; I wondered if other people would be looking at me, wondering why I wasn't. Thinking I was heartless, maybe. But it wasn't that I was heartless. It wasn't that at all. Valentine and I had never been close to anybody who had died before, and the funny thing was that even though I had never actually met Aunt Theo in real life, I *did* feel close to her. I was confident that I had felt closer to her than Valentine, even though she was the one who was sobbing while I was sitting there on my *Madeline* bed perfectly still.

Clover went on: "I did so want for Aunt Theo to get to meet you and Valentine. But, otherwise, I thought of it more as a *Nice to Have Known You* party, if you see what I mean. Goodbye, farewell—oh, the point of having this party was to bring all of Aunt Theo's friends back together one last time! She'd been resting up all summer long, hoping that she would be well enough to come to New York in August. The last time I spoke to her was just two days ago, in fact. She sounded quite well, I had no idea it was so near the end. But now I wonder—I wonder, Franny. That was just like Aunt Theo. She always believed in acting all chin up, even at the worst of times."

Clover decided that everybody should know what had happened. Why keep it from Aunt Theo's friends, when so many of them were right there? Before she did this, Clover went and "consulted," as she put it, with Cousin Honor. She said that was because Cousin Honor was the only blood relative of Aunt Theo's there. The two of them agreed it would be best to go ahead and break the news to the group. Afterward there were tears and toasts. Cousin Honor chimed in, saying that we were to "open another bottle of champagne if you please and carry on."

"Carry on doing *what?*" demanded Valentine.

"Why," said Cousin Honor bravely, though there were tears in her eyes as well, "for instance, we could do the tango!"

"*The tango?*" Valentine repeated.

Cousin Honor was small, but she reminded me somehow of a queen. She just had *that air.* ("Imperious," Ellery whispered to me. "Honor was always imperious. Just like her cousin Theo.") I watched her, fascinated. Clover and I exchanged glances, wondering if she actually could be serious about us doing the tango at a time like this. Turned out, she was.

"Warren?" she said grandly, putting her hand out to him and leading him in the first dance. Clover shrugged and went to search for some appropriate music to put on among Aunt Theo's old records.

At Cousin Honor's prompting, Alexander and I even tried to do the tango together, though we were not very good at it, either of us. And we were blushing the whole time.

Meanwhile, Valentine did the tango with Laurent Victoire, the auburn-haired Frenchman, who selected her as his dancing partner especially, and who, unlike Alexander and me, turned out to be very, very good at it. By the end of it, Valentine was pretty good at it too, though she did keep bursting into tears every now and then and exclaiming *"Dead, she's dead,"* as if anyone could have forgotten. It wasn't that we had forgotten. It's that we were trying to do what Aunt Theo would have wanted: not to let on. To act chin up, even at the worst of times.

23

That Was the Summer When

*H*ere is Aunt Theo's obituary, which Mom and Dad clipped for us from *The New York Times*. We read it once we were back home in San Francisco, just a couple of days after the night of the party, where we were supposed to get to finally meet her.

THEODORA "THEO" WENTWORTH WHITIN BELL DIES AT 65; RADCLIFFE BEAUTY, AVEDON MODEL & NOVELIST

THEODORA "THEO" WENTWORTH WHITIN BELL, a swan-necked Radcliffe beauty, Avedon model, one-time novelist, and legendary free spirit, died in Germany after a long illness. She was sixty-five.

Ms. Bell (despite countless admirers, she never married) was born in Boston to the famous Bell clan, in a five-story brownstone facing the Vincent Club, to Abbott Wentworth Ford Bell and Victoria Pendleton Theale Whitin. Her ancestors on both sides were painted by John Singer Sargent, and it was said that Ms. Bell's tall, dark chiseled beauty suggested the elegance of another era.

She first made a reputation for being rebellious by getting

kicked out of Miss Wilcox's Academy for Girls in the tenth grade; she refused to show sufficient team spirit during volleyball practice, and encouraged other girls to follow her example. She was admitted to Radcliffe several years later, only to have *Esquire* magazine vote her "the most sought after date in the Ivy League." She was also on the cover of *Mademoiselle*'s "College Girl" issue in 1962. After Radcliffe she was a runway model in Paris. Later on when she moved back to New York she modeled for Richard Avedon. In his series of photographs of her she wears a floor-length black velvet gown and has a stuffed swan perched on her shoulder. The late sixties took her to Hollywood, where she had bit parts in several notable movies of the period.

Some of these adventures appear in her highly autobiographical novel, *Made in Paris* (Random House, 1972).

In more recent years, Ms. Bell kept residences in Greenwich Village, Paris, and Sag Harbor, NY. She was a plucky world traveler and charmed flocks of friends and admirers on two continents. Her witty letters and slashing black handwriting were legendary among her correspondents. "One always looked forward to receiving her letters," said Ellery Jones, a longtime friend of Ms. Bell's and a New York City gossip columnist. "Her writing style was absolutely delicious."

Longtime New Yorkers may recall Ms. Bell as that tall, striking, dark woman who used to conduct tango lessons every Wednesday afternoon in front of the angel at the Bethesda Fountain in Central Park. Her signature outfit when doing the tango was a black chiffon dress and red satin ballet pumps, from the French fashion house Lanvin.

Ms. Bell leaves numerous cousins on both the Bell and Whitin sides, but is survived by no children.

"So that explains why we all did the tango that night!" exclaimed Valentine on reading this.

"The tango?" repeated Mom and Dad. "You actually did the tango?"

"Why yes, let me show you," said Valentine, and struck a Spanish-style pose.

A couple of months after this, I got a package from Clover.

Dear Franny,

Now that Theo's dead, maybe you'll know why I agreed to meet Digby for that foolish sentimental lunch at the Oyster Bar last summer. I'll tell you: because I knew that Theo was dying and he was a link to what remained of my girlhood, my past. (Which is also why I was such a wreck when Carlo, my little turtle, died, if you remember. Weeping over a turtle at MY advanced age!) Now, I'm afraid, nothing remains of my past at all. But I'm so happy to have my memories of you and Valentine this past summer. I told you girls once that there will always be "one summer" you'll remember. Now I have two!

I hope you find the enclosed pretty. I made it just for you, Franny, with your own style of beauty in mind.

All my love,
Clover

Inside the package there was a dear little box, two bluish-pink oyster shells with a tiny gold hinge. A jewelry box! How sweet of Clover. All my life I hoped to be able to look at it and think to myself those ravishing words: *That was the summer when—*

Epilogue
Boucher's *Seasons*

*T*hree years later I'm visiting New York City again.

Now, at seventeen, I've come East to look at schools; my first choice is Sarah Lawrence. I thought of going to Bennington, like Clover, but I just don't think I could stand being in Vermont. I'm still a city girl. I also came to New York to visit Val, who is now a junior at Barnard.

Val is dating someone new—she's always dating someone new, or so it seems to me—and I have a boyfriend back in San Francisco I met at music camp. After that summer in New York, our parents sent us straight back to that camp—no more adventures for a while. But something had happened to me that summer and forever afterward I knew I didn't want to be a singer; after coming back from New York, I wanted to be a writer. What had happened to Valentine eventually happened to me. I filled out, rejected the pixie cut Clover had insisted I get that summer, and grew my hair long again. Even if it is not quite as "sophisticated" long, Teddy—my boyfriend—likes running his fingers through it, and I'm at the age where things like that are much more important to me.

Anyway, after that summer in New York, I kept on "taking notes." Sometimes when I think back to that summer, it seems like all the big things that happened happened not to me but to Valentine, and I suppose in a way they did. But then I remember something that Clover once told us, that afternoon at the Frick, that "a true Romantic knows that the inner life is the thing, the only thing that really matters, in the end." If that's true—that the inner life is the only thing that matters—then everything I remember about that summer will always play a big part in mine. I remember Clover telling us that happiness is the most fragile thing in the world.

And as for my sister, Valentine—but how am I to know about Valentine? What started to happen that summer is finally complete. We're not close anymore. You can still spend time with someone—you can still have a lot of fun with them, even—without being close. Being close is different.

In her will, Aunt Theo left us a modest amount of money, which we can use once we're twenty-one. It isn't a lot of money. Clover said she wanted us to think of it as traveling money, for us to go off and have some adventures with. She said Aunt Theo believed in the necessity of women leading "large lives." Aunt Theo also left me her book collection. She left Valentine that nude portrait of her that was painted one morning in Paris when she was a young woman and the red satin Lanvin ballet pumps she used to do the tango in, after learning from Clover that they wore the same shoe size. And Valentine actually *wears* them sometimes, not caring if they get ruined. If they were mine, I wouldn't wear them ever. But that's the difference between Valentine and me.

Valentine hasn't gone on the stage. She's an art history major; she's doing her thesis on Boucher's *Seasons*, which we first saw at the Frick with Clover that summer. Clover? We don't see or hear much from Clover anymore. After Aunt Theo died, she left Clover most of her money, including her apartment in the Village. But last I heard she had sold the apartment and was living abroad, out of her orange Hermès suitcase. She used to send us postcards sometimes, then they petered out. Oh, but I'm lying. We used to write back but then one day we stopped. We got swept up in our own lives.

We got swept back up also into the modern world. It was as if, once we left Aunt Theo's apartment, we shed some kind of magical golden skin that had protected us. When we left there, the edges of things just never felt quite so soft ever again.

And another thing: I never write real letters to anyone anymore, though I miss them. There was also a time after we went back to San Francisco when Alexander and I wrote postcards, and I kept the ones he sent me and showed them to all my friends. They were very impressed because hardly anybody sends real mail anymore. But then we stopped and all that seems a long time ago now.

And Val? Well, absolutely everybody calls Val Valentine at this point. She always wears her hair pinned up and it isn't so bright red anymore anyway—it's more like what you'd call auburn. And another thing is when I look at her now I no longer think that her eyes are violet. I see what Mom means about them being just plain dark blue. Which makes me wonder, actually, about a lot of things, a lot of other things I might have gotten wrong, might have made more otherworldly and fabulous than they actually ever were. Or does it? Was I so very wrong? Because it also makes me think of that incredibly hot, bright green afternoon when Clover and I strolled through Central Park and went to see *Calder's Circus* at the Whitney—and how *Calder's Circus* freezes some of that preciousness in miniature: how when you look at it you could be a child again, you could believe that your beautiful older sister's eyes were really and truly the color violet. Violet is *still* one of my favorite words.

These days, if you saw Valentine on the street, you wouldn't be surprised to learn that she was born in Paris; she has something of the Continental air. I don't know how she did it, but she has turned into the sort of woman who knows how to tie a scarf and understands the allure of silence.

Woman, not girl. She's the kind of twenty-year-old you'd take for twenty-five.

One day after hanging out in Valentine's dorm room, we decided to take the subway downtown. We got off in the Village, not far from the building on Lower Fifth where Aunt Theo's old apartment used to be. It was so strange to think of that apartment existing without her. What had happened to the secret roof-deck, the terra-cotta pots, and the lemon trees? We stopped at Caffe Reggio—we take our coffee black now but can't resist the opportunity to have it piled high with whipped cream if it's available—and then decided to go and walk around the Village. It was one of those fall days in Manhattan when everyone is so grateful that the heat has lifted that it's as if the whole city experiences this brief, collective happiness.

"That summer," said Valentine. "Can you believe that we

actually weren't allowed to wear jeans that summer? It just seems so incredible to think of now!"

"Trousers," I said, remembering. "Clover specifically said that Aunt Theo didn't care for women in trousers."

"Trousers!" squealed Valentine. "Trousers!" It had been years since we had heard that word. We laughed and laughed just at the thought of it.

"That summer . . ." said Valentine again, and there was something a little serious about her voice when she said this, and I wondered what was coming. Revelations, I thought.

"What about that summer?" I asked, in a different tone of voice myself.

"Well, it wasn't only first love I learned about that summer." She blushed, and now that she's all grown up it's not like Valentine to blush. Then she asked me: "Oh, Franny. You never even guessed?"

"Guessed what?"

She threw her hands up in the air. She said once again: "Oh, Franny. *My father.*"

It was years since we had mentioned him. I could barely remember the way, when we were still little girls, we used to make up all those bedtime stories about him.

"What about your father?" I said now.

"Why, he came to that party, on the night Aunt Theo died. He came all the way from Paris because Clover invited him. Clover knew, see. That he was my father. Wasn't that thoughtful of her? She wanted us to finally meet."

I felt almost betrayed—only almost—that Clover had never

told me, when all this time I'd thought I was so much closer to Clover that summer than Valentine was. Also, I was disappointed I hadn't guessed any of this, when I thought of myself as being so much more observant than Val. Now it seemed that I hadn't been quite so observant on the night of that party after all.

"Laurent Victoire," she said. "The man who was there from Paris."

"Oh," I said, remembering, "he was the one who painted *L'heure de la lavande* that was over her bed."

"Yes," said Valentine. "Before he fell in love with Mom, years, years before, he was in love with Theo."

"Everybody was," I said.

"Yes, I guess so. But Mom met him through Aunt Theo, in fact. The two of them had stayed friends. But it was Theo, Clover said, who took care of Mom and me when I was born. Theo bought me all these fancy French baby clothes, remember."

I remembered. I remembered them because after Mom moved to San Francisco and married Dad and I was born, she dressed me in Valentine's French baby clothes. She still has some of those clothes, even now.

"You know," Valentine went on. "Mom told me she still dreams of that apartment sometimes."

"What apartment?"

"The apartment in Paris. Laurent's. It must have been the same one where he painted Aunt Theo, I think. She says it was very beautiful, the most beautiful apartment she was ever inside of in all her life. She says it was rose-colored. *Rose*," repeated Valentine with a sigh, to give emphasis to the image.

And I saw in my imagination a rose-colored Parisian apartment. It was as if I had been there before, in another life, and that made sense because my mother had.

I didn't feel hurt or angry that Val had known more than I did. No, the main thing I felt was: *curious.*

"Who knows? Maybe he'll invite me to stay in that apartment in Paris someday . . ." Valentine was saying now.

Life is so rich, I thought to myself. It was so rich that you missed out on things even when you thought you were so good at paying attention. For some reason after I had this thought, I wanted to go back to Val's dorm room and start writing down a new story. There were so many stories I wanted to tell and I was excited about all of them.

I'm happy, I thought, and told myself to try to remember this moment before it was gone. This is what Clover meant.

Then all of a sudden, there we were standing in the park just in front of the Washington Square Arch, near the same spot where we used to go and have picnics sometimes, when a man stopped us and asked Valentine: "Excuse me. Are you a ballerina?"

I didn't blame him for thinking it. Val was wearing a black cashmere pullover and pony-skin slippers, and then there's something about the way she stands these days. She's grown into her legs and she's not as jumpy, not as expressive, as before.

Val paused. What she said surprised me: "I was."

The man said: "Oh. Thought so. Are you dancing in anything now?"

Then Val laughed lightly and said: "No. I meant I was a ballerina years, years ago."

"When?" the man said. He leaned toward her; I think it was her air of slight sadness that captured him.

"One summer," said Val. "One beautiful summer."

And heads held high we both walked on, through the Arch, into that rich and marvelous New York City light.